FR...
NANCY DREW FILES

THE CASE: Nancy tries to find out who is sending the deadly valentines and dark threats to the students of Theta Pi.

CONTACT: When Kristin Seidel, president of Theta Pi, asks Nancy to investigate, she doesn't know she's extending an invitation to danger.

SUSPECTS: Tamara Carlson—*She was dying to be campus sweetheart, but would she kill for it as well?*

Casey Thompson—*He thought he was Rosie Lopez's valentine, but she broke his heart. Did dreams of romance lead to a desire for revenge?*

Max Dombrowski—*His daughter tried to pledge Theta Pi, but the sorority turned her away. Did he pledge to make them pay?*

COMPLICATIONS: The Valentine's Day Ball is the climax of Sweetheart Week, and Nancy and Ned intend to dance the evening away . . . as long as a third party doesn't outbid Ned for Nancy's affections!

Books in The Nancy Drew Files® Series

Available from ARCHWAY Paperbacks

Case 92
My Deadly Valentine
Carolyn Keene

AN ARCHWAY PAPERBACK
Published by POCKET BOOKS

New York   London   Toronto   Sydney   Tokyo   Singapore

This book is a work of fiction. Names, characters, places and incidents are either products of the author's imagination or are used fictitiously. Any resemblance to actual events or locales or persons, either living or dead, is entirely coincidental.

AN ARCHWAY PAPERBACK *Original*

An Archway Paperback published by
POCKET BOOKS, a division of Simon & Schuster Inc.
1230 Avenue of the Americas, New York, NY 10020

ISBN: 0-671-79484-1

First Archway Paperback printing February 1994

10 9 8 7 6 5 4 3 2 1

Cover art by Cliff Miller

Printed in the U.S.A.

IL 6+

My Deadly Valentine

Chapter

One

Don't you think three valentines is a little excessive for one guy?" Nancy Drew asked her friend Bess Marvin. Nancy put her foot on the brakes of her Mustang, stopped at a red light, and smiled at her friend, who was sitting in the passenger seat. "I think one would have been just fine. You must *really* like Kyle."

The light of a streetlamp shone on Bess's blond hair. "I won't deny it," she said, sighing as she tucked the three cards she had just read to Nancy back in her shoulder bag. "Cupid's hit me hard this time—and I couldn't be happier. For once I'll be celebrating Valentine's Day with a guy I'm crazy about."

Nancy was just as happy as Bess. She was going to spend Sweetheart Week, an Emerson College tradition, with her boyfriend, Ned Nickerson.

1

Kyle Donovan, who worked as a paralegal for Nancy's father, Carson Drew, was planning to join them at Emerson on Friday afternoon.

"Kyle's pretty sure he'll be able to get away early," Bess said.

"I hope my dad doesn't work him too hard this week," Nancy teased. "He'll need all his energy to keep up with you—and Cupid."

The light changed, and Nancy drove a few more blocks. At a sign reading Welcome to Emerson College, Nancy turned onto a tree-lined road that led to the campus.

Although it was almost seven and the weather was freezing, the college was alive with people rushing about. As she drove past the sports complex, Nancy felt a tremor of excitement. Ned was inside that building, warming up for the Tuesday night basketball game. And soon she'd be right there, watching him!

"I'm so glad Kristin invited us to stay at the Theta Pi house," Bess said.

Nancy nodded. She and Bess had met Kristin Seidel during a previous visit to Emerson College. Staying with her at the sorority meant that they'd be in the midst of every Sweetheart Week event.

"Greek Row," Bess said, reading a street sign. "That's it, on the right."

The wide street was lined with majestic old houses, each emblazoned with large Greek letters signifying the sorority or fraternity that was in residence there. The Theta Pi house was a two-story, plantation-style building with thin white pillars gracing the front.

"Oh, look!" Bess exclaimed. "The windows are dotted with hearts. That's so cute," she said as Nancy pulled into the driveway.

After Nancy parked in the small lot behind the house, the girls went to the front entrance and rang the bell. A minute later, the door was opened by a short, pretty girl with chin-length shiny black hair.

Nancy and Bess introduced themselves.

"Kristin's been talking about you guys all day," the girl said. "I'm Mindy Kwong. Come on in."

Nancy and Bess followed Mindy through a spacious formal living room to a doorway on the far left of the room. It led to a den, where half a dozen girls were sitting on the floor or sprawled on slightly worn furniture.

Just then a petite blond scrambled up. Nancy recognized Kristin Seidel, president of Theta Pi, immediately.

Kristin rushed toward them, hopping over an open jar of paint. "You made it in time for the game!" she said, giving Nancy and Bess hugs.

"Wouldn't miss it," Nancy said.

"Nancy's a big fan of one of the players," Bess explained, then giggled.

"I can see why. Ned Nickerson is just about the cutest guy on campus." Kristin glanced at her sorority sisters and pointed to Nancy. "Yes, ladies, this is the girl who's won the heart of the captain of Emerson's basketball team."

"Lucky you!" one of the girls called out.

"Some introduction, huh?" Kristin teased, then announced, "This is Nancy Drew and Bess Marvin. They'll be staying with us this week. And these are a few of my sorority sisters." One by one, she pointed to the girls. "Denise, Whitney, Juanita, Brook, Trish—and you met Mindy."

The girls called out greetings.

"There are eighteen of us living at the house," Kristin went on. "Some of the girls are already over at the gym."

The coffee table was covered with brightly colored paper scraps and bottles of glue, paint, and glitter. "Looks like an art project," Nancy commented.

"We're working on our valentines for the charity auction," Kristin explained. "It's a Theta Pi tradition. We all make valentines. Friday afternoon we'll auction them off to the highest bidder. The money goes to charity, and each girl goes to Saturday's Sweetheart Ball with the guy who bought her valentine."

"Why don't you and Bess join in?" Mindy asked.

"I'd love to," Bess said. "And Kyle should make it here just in time for the auction. My boyfriend is driving out to join us for the weekend," she told Kristin.

"It sounds like fun," Nancy said. "Count me in."

"It's really great of you all to include us in sister activities this week," Bess said.

"It's the least we can do for the detective who saved my skin," Kristin responded.

Nancy had met Kristin while working on a case during Emerson's homecoming week. Kristin had been blamed for a fire that broke out at a pep rally, but Nancy had proved that it wasn't Kristin's fault.

"All I did was bring the facts to light," Nancy said, checking her watch. "Wow. It's already seven-fifteen."

"We'd better get a move on if we want to catch the game," Kristin said. "I'll help you unload your car, and then we'd better get over to the sports complex."

"One of our sisters is going to be crowned Sweetheart in a ceremony right after the game," Mindy explained. "Then there's a party, with refreshments and a deejay playing oldies."

"Just think," Juanita said, "Rosie Lopez, Emerson Sweetheart. I'm so proud of her!"

Kristin helped the girls carry their luggage from Nancy's Mustang to a large bedroom at the top of the stairs. Nancy felt right at home in the cozy room. The wallpaper was patterned with pink cabbage roses, and the windows offered views of Greek Row.

"Hope you don't mind rooming with Mindy

5

and me," Kristin said as she and Mindy dragged two mattresses through the door and put them on the floor.

"It's perfect," Nancy said, shoving her suitcase against a wall.

"I'm so glad you invited us to stay with you," Bess said. She paused in front of a dressing table, and frowned at her reflection. "I'm a mess." She searched through her shoulder bag and found her brush. After quickly brushing her hair, she put on lipstick.

Nancy joined Bess at the mirror. She ran her fingers through her reddish blond hair, then squeezed Bess's arm. "You look great. Let's go!"

Since all the girls of Theta Pi wanted to see their sorority sister crowned Sweetheart Queen, they filed out of the house together, chatting and laughing. Stepping outside, Nancy zipped her turquoise down jacket and turned up her collar. It had to be below freezing, Nancy thought.

As the girls walked along Greek Row, Kristin pointed out the different sorority and fraternity houses. "That's the Omega Chi Epsilon house," Kristin said, grinning mischievously. "Look familiar?"

It was the fraternity house where Ned lived. "We've been to a few parties there," Nancy said, laughing.

"That's the Delta Zeta house." Kristin pointed to a three-story Tudor with a wide entrance flanked by shrubs.

"They're our rivals," Denise added.

"Don't say that, Denise!" Kristin said, giving her friend a playful punch in the arm.

"But it's true," Denise said, pulling her pink mittens over the cuffs of her white jacket. "We're the top two sororities on campus."

"In terms of the number of girls who want to pledge," Kristin clarified. "But we're not really rivals."

"It's more of a personal rivalry," Mindy pointed out. "Rosie and Tamara Carlson, one of the Delta Zeta girls, are always trying to outdo each other."

"That name sounds familiar," Bess said. "Didn't we meet her when we were here last, Nan?"

"Yes," Nancy replied. "I helped clear her boyfriend, Zip, of some false charges. But I only talked with her a few times."

"Anyway," Mindy went on, "I heard that Tamara pitched a fit when Rosie beat her in the Sweetheart competition."

When Kristin gave Mindy a warning look, Mindy just shrugged and giggled. "Can I help it if I love to dish the dirt?" Mindy asked.

Nancy listened to the conversation, but her mind was on Ned. She couldn't wait to see him!

By the time the girls arrived at the sports complex and joined the other Theta Pi sisters in the stands, it was game time. The bleachers were a blur of shaking pom-poms, all purple and orange, the Emerson colors. Down on the court, cheerleaders were revving up the fans, and the whole gym resounded with the sound of stomping feet.

Nancy and Bess joined the crowd, cheering as the players took their positions on the court.

"Let's go, Wildcats!" Bess yelled.

The opening buzzer sounded, and the game began.

Most of the time, Nancy kept her eyes on Ned. His handsome face was tight with determination as he blocked shots and raced up the court. Emerson's team fought hard, but at the end of the first half, the Wildcats were trailing by ten points.

During halftime Nancy recognized one of the cheerleaders, a pretty girl with brown, curly hair, dark skin, and a bright smile.

"Check out that cheerleader, the third one from the left," she said, nudging Bess.

"It's Tamara," Bess said.

"Rosie's nemesis," Kristin said. "When they're in the same room, they fight like cats and dogs."

"Really?" Nancy was surprised. Tamara had seemed nice enough when she had met her.

The second half started with a whir of excitement when Ned got the ball. Nancy jumped up to cheer as he dribbled it to the far end of the court. Hook shot! Basket! Two points! Emerson was just eight points behind!

The other team took the ball but fumbled it.

Ned scooped up the ball and passed it to a teammate, a lanky guy with thick blond hair that was pulled back in a ponytail. He caught Ned's pass, lobbed the ball at the basket, and—swish!

"He's good," Bess said.

"That's Casey Thompson," Kristin explained. "He and Rosie have been dating for a few months."

Unfortunately, the Emerson team couldn't rally long enough to take the lead. When the final buzzer sounded, the Kingston College fans let out a thunderous victory cheer.

"Oh, well," Kristin sighed as the opposing team's fans filed out of the gym. "We may have lost the game, but we know Rosie's a winner."

Just then the Emerson marching band launched into a song as they came onto the basketball court in a crown-shaped formation. When they finished their routine, the lights in the gym were lowered, and a husky man in a tweed jacket appeared at the microphone. Nancy recognized Dean Jarvis, one of the college's administrators. She'd worked with him on a few cases during past visits to Emerson.

"Ladies and gentlemen," he said, "I am proud to introduce the young lady you have chosen as this year's Emerson Sweetheart, Ms. Rosie Lopez."

There was a drumroll as the official escort, a guy from the band's color guard, walked Rosie to the spotlight. Wearing a burgundy cocktail dress that complemented her dark complexion and curly brown hair, Rosie sparkled with enthusiasm as she thanked everyone.

During Rosie's speech, Nancy's attention wandered to the locker room door. She felt sure that Ned wouldn't want to miss this. And what about Casey, Rosie's boyfriend?

Sure enough, the door swung open, and Nancy spotted Ned and Casey, still wearing their uniforms. They made their way unobtrusively into the gym and stood under the backboard to watch the ceremony.

Dean Jarvis presented Rosie with an engraved gold locket. Then she was crowned with a glittering rhinestone tiara.

"They use that same crown every year," Kristin explained to Nancy and Bess. "But Rosie gets to keep the locket."

"All right, Rosie!" Kristin shouted, and followed her sorority sisters to the floor of the gym. The Theta Pis swarmed around Rosie, eager to congratulate her.

"I'll be right back," Nancy told Bess. She raced down the bleachers and made her way through the crowd toward Ned.

His face lit up when he spotted her. "Hey, gorgeous!" He rushed forward and swept her off her feet. "You made it!"

Nancy kissed Ned and gave him a big hug, sweaty uniform and all.

"You guys played a great game," she said.

"I wish Coach Elliot agreed," Ned said. "Fortunately, Casey and I got excused from the postgame speech." He nodded at his teammate, who was pressing into the crowd around Rosie. "He wants to congratulate her, but it doesn't look as if he's having much luck."

Ned was right. Casey couldn't get past the wall of Theta Pis surrounding Rosie. Judging from the scowl on his face, he wasn't too happy about it, either.

"Rosie!" Casey shouted, pushing past Mindy and Kristin. "For once, would you Theta Pis back off?" he snapped.

Kristin raised her eyebrows and stood back.

From the ruddy color of Casey's face, Nancy could tell he was getting madder by the second.

Just then Rosie swung around.

The happy buzz of the crowd died as curious faces turned to the couple.

At first a distressed look filled Rosie's brown eyes. Then she shook her head and said icily, "You don't own me, Casey Thompson, and if you're going to pick on my sisters, you can take a hike."

"But, Rosie—" Casey argued.

"You've got no right being rude to my friends," she said, cutting him off. "I mean it. Get lost!"

Casey was fuming now. "You'll be sorry you said that, Rosie Lopez."

Chapter

Two

ROSIE DIDN'T REPLY but stood her ground.

Then Casey mumbled something Nancy couldn't understand and stormed into the locker room.

"You'd better go talk to him," Nancy told Ned. She was surprised that the argument between Rosie and Casey had exploded into a breakup. But Ned was a diplomat. He had a talent for soothing wounded egos. Maybe he could help Casey.

After Ned ducked into the locker room, Nancy found Bess at the foot of the bleachers.

"What was all the commotion?" Bess asked. "I could see that something was wrong, but I couldn't hear a thing."

Nancy described the argument. "She told Casey to take a hike—literally."

"That's too bad," Bess said. "This should be the perfect moment for Rosie. I mean, how often does a girl get crowned Sweetheart?"

It was true. But when Nancy glanced over at Rosie, she was surprised to see that the girl didn't seem too upset. She was still hugging her sorority sisters.

By now tables had been set up around the edge of the gym. Platters of baked goods were being arranged on them as the deejay tested the sound system. "This one's dedicated to Rosie Lopez, Emerson's Sweetheart," he said, turning up the volume for the first song.

A few students start to dance. Nancy noticed that Rosie and the other Theta Pis were headed toward one of the refreshment tables. "Let's go over and get something to drink," she suggested.

"And maybe a doughnut," Bess said, eyeing one table.

Nancy and Bess were sipping hot cider when Kristin and Rosie joined them. "Rosie Lopez, meet Nancy and Bess," Kristin said, turning to her sorority sister. "They'll be staying with us during Sweetheart Week."

"Great!" Rosie replied.

"Nice to meet you," Nancy said.

"Congratulations." Bess was beaming. "You make a beautiful Sweetheart."

"Thanks." Dimples appeared in Rosie's cheeks as she smiled. "It's a major thrill."

Just then Ned appeared at Nancy's side. His

hair was still damp from the shower, and he'd changed into jeans and a cotton sweater. His jacket and knapsack were slung over his shoulder.

"Hiya, Bess!" Ned planted a kiss on Bess's cheek, then turned to Rosie. "Congrats. Sorry your boyfriend isn't here to celebrate with you."

"He's not my boyfriend anymore," Rosie said softly.

"Casey's just wired," Ned explained. "Winning this game was important to him. When things weren't going his way afterward, well . . . he lost it. No excuse, but I'm sure he'll apologize in the morning."

"Isn't he coming to the party?" Nancy asked.

Ned shook his head. "He blew out of the locker room in a rage. Didn't even stop to shower or change out of his uniform."

"Another tantrum!" Rosie rolled her eyes.

"Sounds like he was really ticked off," Kristin said, squeezing Rosie's arm.

Rosie frowned and stared down at the ground as if she didn't want anyone to know how much Casey had hurt her. Nancy felt bad for her. She sensed that Rosie's harsh attitude toward Casey was all bravado.

"I can't deal with his temper anymore," Rosie said. "When I told him to get lost, I meant it. It's over between us."

"Oh, no," Bess said sympathetically.

Nancy gave Bess a warning look. Her best

friend loved playing matchmaker, but this was something that Casey and Rosie needed to work out for themselves.

"Anyone else want to hit the refreshment table?" Nancy suggested, changing the subject.

"I'm game," said Ned. "A guy works up an appetite running up and down the court. Just give me a second to throw my things on the bleachers."

By the time they sampled the doughnuts, cakes, and heart-shaped cookies, the party was in full swing. An old rock and roll hit was playing, and across the gym students were dancing. Kristin came off the dance floor dragging a husky guy with dark eyes and jet black hair combed back from his forehead.

"You've worn me out, Fitz," she told him, then turned to Nancy and Bess. "Anybody want to dance with my friend Mike Fitzgerald?"

Bess was already tapping her foot to the beat, and Nancy gave her a playful shove. "Go on. I'll dance with Ned."

"Let's go!" Bess said, hurrying away with the guy Kristin had called Fitz.

As Kristin went over to the snack table, Ned leaned down to whisper in Nancy's ear. "Are we going to join them? Or are you just going to stand there looking beautiful?"

Nancy laughed. "Tough choice. But since we don't get to see too much of each other these days, why don't we dance?"

A ballad was starting up just as they walked toward the dance floor. It gave Nancy a great excuse to cuddle close to Ned. She loved being in his arms, leaning her head on his warm, solid shoulder.

All too soon the ballad faded to another rock and roll standard. Nancy and Ned tried out a few jitterbug steps, and Nancy laughed when he swung her around.

After the song ended, they met Bess, Kristin, and Fitz by the punch bowl. As they waited for cool drinks, Kristin introduced Fitz to Ned and the girls.

"Don't you guys know each other?" Bess asked.

Ned shook his head. "Emerson's pretty big," he said. "Where do you hang out?" he asked Fitz.

"Fitz is like a fixture around the Theta Pi house," Kristin answered as she pushed her blond bangs off her forehead. "He's a lifesaver. He fixes things and tutors some of the girls in chemistry. Fitz is everybody's big brother. And when he's not hanging out with us, he practically runs the student union." She patted the solidly built guy on the back.

A wide smile softened Fitz's face. "Better stop now before I get a swelled head.

"It sounds like the Theta Pis appreciate your help," Nancy said.

"They're a great bunch," Fitz said, waving at

someone across the gym. "Excuse me," he told the group, "but I think Emerson's Sweetheart needs a dance partner." He finished his punch in one swallow, then darted away.

"I hope all you Theta Pis are planning to attend the Sweetheart Ball," Ned told Kristin. "I have a personal interest, since it's sponsored by my frat. We've been working hard to pull it all together. We want a huge turnout. It's open to the whole student body," he explained to Nancy.

"I think it's going to be extra romantic this year," Bess said. "Especially since Valentine's Day actually falls on Saturday."

"We're looking forward to it," Kristin told Ned. "And don't forget about the Theta Pi auction on Friday afternoon. We're going to auction off Nancy's valentine—and you know what that means."

"Really?" Ned clapped a hand to his forehead. "That's going to cost me a bundle."

"It's for a good cause," Nancy said, squeezing Ned's arm. "And you'd better come up with the money. I can't imagine going to the Sweetheart Ball with anyone but you."

"I'm auctioning off a valentine, too," Bess announced. "But I sure hope Kyle makes it to the auction in time to bid on it."

"If not, I'll be his proxy," Ned volunteered. "Though I can see this conversation is getting more expensive by the minute."

"We're worth it," Nancy said, leaning up to kiss Ned's cheek.

It was after midnight when the crowd began to thin out. After one last slow dance, Nancy and Ned went to pick up their jackets on the bleachers, where Bess was sitting with Kristin.

"I hate to end the fun, but I've got classes in the morning," Ned said as he tugged on his jacket and slung his knapsack over his shoulder.

"No problem." Kristin pulled on her coat.

Bess yawned. "Besides, it's only Tuesday. We've got the whole week to play."

"Party animal!" Nancy teased.

Bundled up in jackets, scarves, and gloves, they filed out of the sports complex into the cold night air.

With her arm linked through Ned's, Nancy enjoyed the walk through the campus. They passed the modern glass-sided library, then took the path toward the student union, which was built into the hill. Two students crossed in front of them, heading for the main entrance of the building. Nancy and her friends continued on, taking a walkway that curved down around the side of the union.

"The student union must be open late," Nancy commented.

"The snack bar and laundromat stay open until three," Kristin explained.

When they came around the back of the building, Nancy saw the lower stories of the student union. At the very bottom of the hill, the path cut through a garden.

"This garden looks so different in the spring when everything's in bloom," Nancy said. The grass was frozen and stubby, and the area was bare except for a few scraggly shrubs and trees.

"They've even turned off the fountain," Bess said. "I guess it would have frozen otherwise."

"It's pretty bleak," Kristin agreed, "but the whole campus looks great after a snowfall."

"Snow's predicted for this week," Ned said as they walked along the path through the garden.

"Snow would be . . ." Nancy's voice trailed off as an object behind the fountain caught her eye. It looked like a hand lying on the ground—but it couldn't be. Maybe it was a glove.

"Nancy?" Ned asked when she stopped walking. "Something wrong?"

But Nancy was already off the path, crossing the grass to look behind the fountain.

Her pulse began to pound as she circled the fountain and saw that she had been right—a body, one arm outstretched, was lying on the ground!

Chapter

Three

NED GASPED as he saw the body.

Kristin and Bess were right behind him. "It's Rosie!" Kristin exclaimed. "What happened to her mouth?"

It had been covered with black tape. Probably to keep her from screaming, Nancy thought. She knelt on the cold ground and eased the tape off. A white scrap of paper was pinned to Rosie's coat, but Nancy ignored it for the moment. She wrapped her fingers around the girl's wrist.

"Oh, no!" Bess cried. "Is she . . . dead?"

"She's got a pulse," Nancy answered, "but we have to call an ambulance."

"There's a pay phone just inside the union," Kristin said, backing away.

"I'll go with you," Bess volunteered.

Nancy watched the two girls run up the hill,

then sat back on her heels to check out Rosie's injuries.

From the trickle of dried blood in Rosie's hair, it appeared that she'd been hit on the head. Nancy could see that she was breathing normally, but her face was ashen. "We've got to elevate her feet," Nancy told Ned.

He looked around, then slipped the knapsack off his shoulder. "This should do it." Gently, he lifted Rosie's feet and tucked the knapsack under them.

As he did, Nancy noticed something on the heels of Rosie's shoes. "Look at this," she said, carefully lifting a foot again. The cream-colored suede heels were smudged with black streaks. "It's some kind of soot," Nancy said.

"Could be dirt from the garden," Ned guessed.

Nancy nodded. "But see how the dirt runs up the shoe's heel? She was dragged. Probably attacked someplace else, then brought here."

Nancy looked at the note that was pinned to Rosie's lapel. In the light from one of the overhead lamps that dotted the campus, Nancy read it aloud: "'You will pay for the heart you broke.'" The note was signed "Cupid."

Ned shook his head. "Sounds like a sicko with a vendetta."

"Or an angry boyfriend," Nancy said.

The note was attached to Rosie's coat by a safety pin. Nancy studied the handwriting. Wide, square, block-printed letters—not as easy to identify as script. Carefully, with her gloves she turned the white slip of paper over and was surprised to find part of a printed diagram on the back. "Check this out," she said.

Ned glanced over her shoulder. "It looks like a wiring diagram," he said.

"'Heating-Cooling Subbase,'" Nancy read the captions aloud. "'Fan Relay. Contactor Coil.'" She glanced up at Ned. "Sounds like a diagram for some type of furnace."

"It's a strange piece of evidence," Ned said.

Nancy nodded. "The police will definitely want it." Just then Bess and Kristin appeared at the bend in the footpath.

"The ambulance is on its way," Bess shouted, her breath forming puffs of mist. "We called the police, too." As the girls joined them at Rosie's side, Nancy rubbed the girl's hands between her own, trying to keep her warm.

"Oh, Rosie," Kristin said, thinking aloud. "Who did this to you?"

"If all goes well, she'll recover completely," Nancy said. "Then she can tell us who attacked her."

In the distance, the wail of sirens cut through the night air. "They'll be here soon," Nancy said, glancing up at Kristin. "In the meantime, talk to her. The sound of your voice might draw her out of her unconscious state."

Nancy gave Bess the job of massaging Rosie's

hands. Then Nancy stood up and nodded at Ned. "Let's search the area for clues."

They circled Rosie's body, looking for footprints, drag marks, or any loose objects, although Nancy knew that the lamplight probably wasn't bright enough to reveal anything significant.

She and Ned combed the garden all the way to the wall of the building, where she noticed a steel door. "Where does this lead?" she called to Kristin.

Kristin looked up and shrugged. "I'm not sure. Probably to an office or conference room on the ground floor of the union."

Nancy tried the knob, but the door was locked tight. What was on the other side? she wondered.

"Any idea who might have done this?" Ned asked her as they continued combing the area.

Nancy sighed, realizing that Ned wouldn't want to hear the answer. "I know he's your friend, but considering the note, the most obvious guess is Casey Thompson."

"Casey's not a bad guy," Ned said forcefully. "Okay, so he was mad when he left the locker room—but do you really think he'd do this to Rosie?"

"Maybe it was a crime of passion," Nancy said. "He was upset about losing the game. He was mad at Rosie. She told him to take a hike. And didn't she say something about his temper? Apparently tonight wasn't the first time Casey's flown off the handle."

"The guy does have a short fuse," Ned admitted. "I know that much from being his teammate."

Their conversation was interrupted by the arrival of an ambulance, escorted by a campus police officer. The vehicles pulled to a stop in the small lot beyond the garden. Dean Jarvis arrived a minute later, huffing and puffing from jogging across campus.

"A student has been injured," Nancy said, standing back to give the medical squad room. She pointed out the note to the campus security guard, who carefully unpinned it and placed it in a handkerchief.

Everyone watched silently as the paramedics loaded Rosie onto a stretcher. The medics lifted the gurney into the back of the ambulance, then got inside and closed the doors. The van rolled down the campus lane toward the hospital, its red lights flashing.

"We're lucky you found her," Dean Jarvis told Nancy and Ned. "No one can survive these freezing temperatures for long." He rubbed his gloved hands together briskly. "Now, let's gather whatever evidence we can find out here," he said to both the campus policeman and Nancy and her friends. "Then we'll head into the union and wait for the Emersonville police."

Forty-five minutes later Nancy, Ned, Kristin, and Bess sat in the pit, a sunken lounge inside the student union. A few students trickled in and out of the building. Some stopped to stare at the cluster of police before they moved on.

The teens had been questioned by Dean Jarvis, the campus security staff, and the Emersonville police.

The black tape from Rosie's mouth and the Cupid's note were collected as evidence by the police. Their search of the crime scene had turned up nothing, although Nancy suggested that they send someone to the hospital to get Rosie's shoes.

"Okay," Emersonville Police Sergeant Weinberg said as he launched into a review of the evidence. "We have reason to believe the victim was attacked elsewhere, then dragged to the garden. And these young people witnessed an argument between the victim and her boyfriend, Casey Thompson."

"That about sums it up," Dean Jarvis said.

"We'll interview this Casey Thompson first thing in the morning," Weinberg told Dean Jarvis.

"Thank you, Sergeant," the dean said. "I'm really hoping that Rosie will be able to identify her attacker. But please keep my office updated."

As the police and campus security began to clear out, Dean Jarvis turned to Nancy. "And I assume *you'll* notify me about any progress you make," he said firmly.

Nancy smiled as she zipped up her parka. "What makes you think I'm going to investigate?" she asked, her eyes twinkling.

"There was never a doubt in my mind, Nancy," he said with a wry smile.

Nancy nodded. "If I learn anything, I'll let you know," she promised.

Tired and somber, the teens went back out into the cold night and returned to the Theta Pi house. Bess and Kristin went inside, while Nancy stayed outside to say good night to Ned.

"I have classes all morning and one in the afternoon," Ned told her, "but I can meet you in between for lunch."

"Sounds good," Nancy said. "Where should we meet?"

"How about at the student union snack bar around noon?" Ned suggested.

"See you then," Nancy said, and kissed Ned goodnight.

Nancy went inside and climbed the stairs of the dark, quiet sorority house. Everyone else had gone to bed, which was just as well, she thought. The news about Rosie would wait until morning. Maybe by then they would have word from the hospital that she was conscious and feeling fine.

As she crawled into bed, Nancy hoped for the best. But she had trouble falling asleep with so many questions nagging at her.

I wonder where Cupid got the paper for his note, she thought as she rolled over. The block printing would be hard to trace, but the diagram wouldn't. Why would someone hurt Rosie? Had anyone else seen the attack? And what did "Cupid" really want?

"I can't believe it! I just can't believe it!" Mindy shook her head as she placed a platter of cinnamon toast on the kitchen table.

Bess and Nancy were eating breakfast along with Mindy and Brook, who had kitchen duty that morning. Kristin was on the phone, talking to the hospital. A few other girls had passed through earlier, before their Wednesday morning classes. Everyone was stunned and alarmed when they heard what had happened to Rosie. Several of the sisters wondered if Casey could be responsible.

Kristin hung up the kitchen phone. "The nurse on Rosie's floor says that she regained consciousness last night, but she's asleep right now."

"What about injuries?" Nancy asked.

"Her arm is broken, and she has a concussion," Kristin answered, pouring a glass of orange juice.

"Thank goodness it's not worse," Bess said.

"A concussion can be pretty serious," Nancy pointed out. "They'll have to observe her for a few days."

"Poor Rosie," Mindy said. "But *you* don't believe Casey would hurt Rosie, do you?" she continued, passing a platter of eggs. "First, he was her boyfriend. He's crazy about Rosie. And second, he left the gym hours before she did."

Nancy served herself some eggs. It was possible that Casey had lain in wait for Rosie to come along. But most girls didn't travel across campus alone at night. "Does anyone remember what time Rosie left the party?" Nancy asked. "And did she leave by herself?"

"I saw her leave just before midnight," Brook said. "She was with Fitz."

"The police will want to question him," Nancy said. She would have to notify Dean Jarvis.

"Wait a minute," Kristin said. "You're not saying that Fitz could have hurt Rosie, are you?"

"It's possible," Nancy said.

"No way!" Brook said.

"Fitz is like our brother," Mindy added. "He's not the guy the police should be grilling."

"But he may have been the last person to see Rosie before the attack," Bess pointed out.

"This whole thing gives me the creeps." Kristin stared at her plate before turning her hazel eyes on Nancy. "I know this is supposed to be your vacation, but could you do a little investigating?"

"You'd have an edge over the police since you're right here on campus," Brook pointed out.

Nancy nodded.

"I just hope that Rosie will be able to identify her attacker," Bess said. "Then the mystery will be solved."

"In the meantime," Nancy said, "does anybody have any idea who might want to hurt Rosie?"

"The whole thing seems pretty obvious to me," Mindy said. "Think about it. Rosie was injured just after she was crowned. Now it sounds as if she won't be out of the hospital in time for the Sweetheart Ball, which means the first runner-up will become Sweetheart. And that just happens to be Tamara Carlson, Rosie's rival from Delta Zeta!"

"But the note sounds like it came from an old boyfriend," Bess pointed out. "Cupid . . . and a broken heart."

"Could be a smoke screen," Mindy persisted. "There's bad blood between them, and Tamara can be vicious."

"Tamara Carlson—vicious?" Bess asked. She and Nancy exchanged a look of disbelief.

Mindy nodded. "Do you know her?"

"We've met her," Nancy said, shrugging. "Another time when we were here. She never seemed vicious to me."

Bess nodded in agreement.

"Well," Mindy said, "let me give you a juicy example. Last week we were eating in the dining hall when word came over the P.A. system that Rosie had won the Sweethcart election. Tamara was fuming. When Rosie got up to bus her tray, Tamara stuck out her foot and tripped her. Dishes shattered, and Rosie fell flat on the floor."

"That sounds pretty nasty," Bess said.

Nancy agreed, and decided to have a talk with Tamara.

The opportunity came sooner than Nancy had expected. At noon she and Bess walked into the student union snack bar, looking for Ned. Instead Nancy spotted Tamara Carlson moving through the line.

"Why don't you grab us a table?" Nancy murmured to Bess. "I'll be right back."

She joined Tamara in line and tapped her on the shoulder. "Tamara, remember me?"

The girl studied Nancy, then she smiled. "You're the detective, right?"

"Nancy Drew. I'm here to spend Sweetheart Week with my boyfriend," Nancy explained, trying to set Tamara at ease.

"That's nice," the girl said, sliding a slice of pie onto her tray. "But aren't you investigating the attack on Rosie Lopez?"

Nancy glanced away. News traveled fast on a college campus. "Not officially," she answered. "What do you know about it?"

"Just that she's in the hospital." Tamara paid the cashier, then turned to Nancy. "I'm sorry about what happened to Rosie. It sounds awful. But I admit, I want to be the next Sweetheart. Her bad luck could be my big break." She turned and walked to a table.

Nancy followed her. The chairs at the table were covered with Delta Zeta jackets.

"Just one more question," Nancy said before Tamara had a chance to pull out a chair and sit down. "Where were you last night after the party, say, after eleven-thirty?"

Tamara's face puckered in anger. "What is this—an interrogation?"

"No." Nancy was surprised by Tamara's tone, but she wasn't backing off. "It's just a simple question."

"Tell her what I was doing last night," Tamara said, glancing at her sorority sisters, who were just arriving at the table with their food-laden trays.

"Last night?" one Delta girl with pale blond hair piped up. "Wasn't that when—"

"I was holed up in the kitchen, studying for that history exam," Tamara insisted.

The blond girl seemed confused for a second. She glanced toward Tamara, then said, "Oh, yeah. That's right."

The other Delta sisters nodded like robots.

I've hit a wall, Nancy thought. If Tamara was lying, she'd never get it out of any of the Delta Zetas!

Chapter

Four

"WHAT'S THE MATTER?" Bess asked when Nancy joined her at the table.

Nancy told Bess about her conversation with Tamara Carlson. "She has a strong motive," Nancy said finally, "and her alibi is flimsy. I don't believe her, though I can't prove that the Deltas are covering for her."

"Wow!" Bess exclaimed. "It's hard to imagine Tamara attacking Rosie."

"That's true," Nancy said, glancing back at the Deltas. "But there's definitely a problem between them. I've got to find out what Tamara was really doing last night."

"In the meantime, Cupid's still on the loose."

"Let's hope he doesn't strike again," Nancy said. "But that reminds me—remember the note from Cupid?" When Bess nodded, Nancy continued. "It was written on the back of a wiring diagram. If I can track down where that diagram came from, I'm one step closer to Cupid."

"Where would you find a wiring diagram?" Bess wondered aloud.

"In an engineering textbook," Nancy suggested. "Or a maintenance manual. That's why I want to check out every inch of this building." The previous night's police search had not gone beyond the garden.

Just then Nancy caught sight of Ned in the doorway of the snack bar. She waved him over. When he reached the table, he dropped his knapsack onto a chair.

"How did your classes go?" Nancy asked him.

"Fine," Ned said, smiling down at the girls. "But I've worked up a major appetite. Let's eat!"

They made their way through the line at the snack bar, putting burgers, fries, and salads on their trays. As they sat down at the table and started eating, Ned asked about Rosie.

Bess gave him an update on the girl's condition, adding, "The Theta Pis asked Nancy to investigate, and of course she agreed."

"That doesn't surprise me," Ned said, grinning at Nancy. "Any leads so far?"

"Well," Nancy said, "I've spoken to Tamara Carlson, who's thrilled at the prospect of becoming Sweetheart now that Rosie's in the hospital.

She has a motive, but I'm not sure about her alibi. I found out that Fitz was the last person seen with Rosie. I need to get the details from him. And then there's Rosie's boyfriend—"

"Who's standing in line even as we speak," Ned said. "Let's see if he'll join us."

When Casey left the snack bar with a bag of food, Ned caught his attention. "Pull up a chair," he told his teammate.

"Okay," Casey said. His blond hair hung loose around his shoulders, and he looked tired as he shrugged off his team jacket.

"Rough night?" Ned asked.

"I'll say." Casey pulled a wrapped sandwich and french fries out of the paper bag. "I was going to eat in my room in the dorm. All morning I've been getting the cold shoulder. Everyone has heard what happened to Rosie last night, and apparently I'm guilty until proven innocent."

"Did you talk to the police?" Nancy asked.

Casey nodded. "They came to the dorm early this morning." He bit into a french fry. "They told me to stay away from her completely. No phone calls, letters, or visits. I guess Rosie and I picked a lousy time to argue. If I'd been with her, maybe none of this would have happened . . ."

"But last night it was clear that you were mad at her," Nancy pointed out.

"Not at *her,*" Casey said. "I was ticked off at that sorority—and I still am. The Theta Pis caused the friction between Rosie and me.

They're always demanding Rosie's time for meetings and rushes and parties."

"It's part of sorority life," Bess said.

"Yeah," Casey replied, "but sometimes they go overboard. It was getting to the point where Rosie and I never had a chance to be alone."

Nancy wondered if Rosie had been using the sorority to put some distance between herself and Casey. Maybe Rosie's interest in him was fading. In any case, the guy clearly held a grudge against the sorority.

"Where did you go last night after you left the sports complex?" Nancy asked him.

"I went ballistic." Casey frowned. "I jumped in my car and hit the road. I spent a few hours pumping quarters into a video machine at an arcade downtown."

"What's the place called?" Nancy asked.

"The Video Zone," Casey said. "You know it, Nickerson."

"Sure." Ned nodded. "Just off Main Street."

As they finished eating, Ned tried to cheer up his teammate, but Casey's mood didn't change.

"I've got another class," Ned said, checking his watch as they stacked their trays.

"Me, too," said Casey.

"What are you girls doing this afternoon?" Ned asked.

"Research," Nancy said cryptically. "Which reminds me. Where's the engineering department?"

"Emerson doesn't have one," Ned told her.

I guess that rules out an engineering textbook, Nancy thought.

"I'll catch you later," Ned said. "Are we still on for the Sweetheart Feature tonight?"

Nancy had forgotten about the romantic movie that would be shown as part of Sweetheart Week. "I wouldn't miss it for the world," she said.

"I'll pick you up at seven-thirty." Ned dropped a kiss on Nancy's cheek, then followed Casey out of the snack bar.

As soon as the guys had left, Nancy turned to Bess. "Let's find a phone," she said, gesturing toward the lobby. "We have some calls to make."

There was a row of pay phones opposite the bookstore. While Nancy placed her calls, Bess went off to browse through the shop.

Nancy's first call was to Dean Jarvis. She told him that Rosie had left the party with Mike Fitzgerald.

"I'll have the police question him," the dean said. "Maybe he can fill us in on the events leading up to the attack."

After the dean hung up, Nancy pulled a phone book onto the shelf. She looked up the number of the Video Zone and dialed it.

"I'd like to speak to whoever was on duty at the arcade last night," Nancy told the guy who answered.

"That'd be Tiger. He's off till Friday. You can try him then."

But today's only Wednesday, Nancy thought, frowning. "I can't wait that long," she said. "Can you give me his home number?"

There was a brief silence on the other end of the line, and then the guy said, "I can't give out an employee's number."

"But this is important," Nancy said firmly.

"Nice try, honey, but we get calls about Tiger all the time. He's got a ton of admirers. Get in line." His tone was slightly snide.

"What?" Nancy asked, confused.

"I can't give you the guy's home number just because you've got a crush on him."

"No," Nancy insisted. "You don't understand. This is about a case I'm—"

"Sorry." The Video Zone employee cut her off. "Call back on Friday." With that, he hung up.

Nancy sighed. She would have to wait to confirm Casey's alibi. She went into the bookshop to find Bess.

"Let's see if Fitz is on duty," Nancy said to her friend. "I want to ask him a few questions about last night, and maybe he can help us check out the building."

From the bookstore clerk Nancy learned that the student union office was on the bottom floor. They were on their way to the ramp when Bess spotted Fitz moving some furniture in the pit.

"Do you do *everything* around here?" Bess teased him.

"Sometimes it feels that way. I'm pretty much paying my own way through school, so I work a lot of hours." He straightened, then climbed out of the pit. "What are you up to today?" he asked cheerfully.

"We're trying to find out what happened to Rosie last night," Bess blurted out.

"Isn't it awful?" Fitz frowned. "I can't help but feel responsible."

"When was the last time you saw her, Fitz?" Nancy asked the husky guy.

He fingered a large key ring he was holding. "Around midnight, I guess. I needed to talk to the night manager."

"Did Rosie come into the building with you?"

Fitz nodded. "But I left her in the lobby and went to the union office. I couldn't have been in there more than five minutes. When I came back, Rosie was gone." He shrugged. "I just assumed she got impatient and left without me. She wasn't in the best of moods after breaking up with Casey."

"Exactly where were you?" Nancy asked.

"First floor, downstairs," Fitz answered.

"Mind if we take a look?" Nancy asked.

"No problem," Fitz said. "In fact, I can give you a tour of the whole building if—"

"Nancy!" someone called.

The girls turned to face the main entrance,

where Kristin was pushing her way past a group of students. Her cheeks, ruddy from running, nearly matched her red ski parka.

"What's up?" Nancy called.

Kristin came to a halt in front of Fitz and the girls. "We just heard from the hospital!"

"Is Rosie okay?" Fitz asked.

"She's wide awake," Kristin said. "And the police have already talked to her about what happened last night!"

Chapter

Five

I WANT TO TALK to Rosie right away," Nancy said excitedly. "This investigation could be wrapped up sooner than anyone expected."

"A bunch of us are driving over to the hospital," Kristin said. "You can ride in my car, if you want. I'm finished with classes for the day, so you can spend as much time as you need."

"That would be great," Nancy said. "Thanks."

"Well, give her my best," Fitz said. "I'd go with you, but I'm on duty here."

"I might still be interested in a tour of the building," Nancy told Fitz as she zipped up her parka. "Can I catch you later this afternoon?"

"I'll be here till four," he said, then waved as the girls hurried out the main door.

* * *

Emersonville's hospital was a gray, three-story building on Main Street. Kristin parked her car two spots down from Juanita, who had brought Brook and Trish in her compact wagon.

The girls braced themselves against the chilly wind and hurried inside. At the main desk, a nurse directed them to a semiprivate room on the second floor. Inside, they found Rosie sitting up in bed, her arm in a plaster cast and sling, her face still a little pale. A nurse stood beside her, checking the intravenous tube.

"Hey, Rosie," Kristin called, knocking on the open door. The girls called out greetings as they spilled into the room and gathered around the bed.

"I'm glad you guys came," Rosie said, forcing a smile.

Suddenly everybody talked at the same time.

"We brought you some clothes," Juanita said.

"You look a little washed out," said Brook.

"When are you coming home?" Trish asked.

Nancy waited as Rosie's sisters chatted with her, trying to cheer her up.

"I want to come home today," Rosie said, nodding at the nurse. "But the doctor has other plans."

"We're running some tests," the nurse said as she made a note on Rosie's chart and hung it on the bottom of the bed. "And the doctor would like to keep you a few days for observation. You can't be too careful with a head injury. I wouldn't plan on returning to school until early next week."

"Next week!" Juanita said as the nurse left.

"I know," Rosie said, frowning. "There goes Sweetheart Week. I could just cry."

The girls exchanged looks of disappointment.

As they continued talking, Nancy went over and picked up Rosie's medical chart. The notes were written in a scrawl, but Nancy managed to decipher them. Rosie had a concussion and a fractured radius, a bone in the lower arm. The doctor had determined that she'd been struck by a "blunt object."

"Is there anything else we can get you while we're here?" Trish offered.

When Rosie asked for some "real food," Juanita, Brook, and Trish offered to run over to a nearby diner. While they made the trip, Nancy, Bess, and Kristin stayed with Rosie.

"Thank goodness you're going to be okay," said Bess, trying to boost Rosie's spirits.

When Rosie glanced down at the cast on her arm, Nancy asked, "Do you remember who did this to you?"

"I never saw the person who attacked me," Rosie explained. "I was in the student union, waiting for Fitz. He was in one of the offices, and I was standing in the lobby when everything went black. Someone must have hit me from behind."

"Do you remember anything? Like being

dragged? Did you see hands, or a blunt weapon?" Nancy probed.

"Nothing." Sadness darkened her brown eyes as she looked up at Nancy. "The police were here this morning. They asked me that, too. They told me that you found me outside, but I have no idea how I got there."

"When you entered the union, was there anyone else around?" Nancy continued.

Rosie frowned. "I think there was a group in the pit, and the lights were on in the snack bar. But I didn't see anyone come into the lobby itself while I was there." She paused. "Of course, I *was* looking at the bulletin board."

Kristin came to Rosie's side. "Nancy's investigating the attack. She's a detective."

"Really?" Rosie's eyes widened. "I could use your help. Somebody really did a number on me. And from the sound of that note the police read to me, I could be in for even more trouble!"

"You're safe for now," Kristin told Rosie, "at least while you're in the hospital."

"But the person who attacked me—that Cupid—has to be stopped," Rosie insisted.

"Do you have any idea who would want to hurt you?" Nancy asked.

"Sure," Rosie said. "Tamara Carlson. And it burns me up to think that she'll be presiding over the Sweetheart Ball while I'm lying here in a hospital bed."

Nancy was surprised by Rosie's vehemence.

43

"Do you think Tamara is strong enough to do this to you?"

"She's a cheerleader, someone who's in good shape," Rosie pointed out.

"What about Casey?" Nancy suggested. "He was pretty mad when you broke up with him. . . ."

"I don't think Casey would hurt me," Rosie said. "The person who knocked me out wanted to get rid of the Emerson Sweetheart." She touched her neck reflexively, then frowned. "My Sweetheart locket," she said. "It's gone!"

"Maybe the nurses took it off when you were admitted," Nancy said.

"I'll go check," Bess volunteered, ducking out of the room. A moment later, she returned with the nurse.

"What's this about missing jewelry?" the nurse asked. She checked Rosie's chart, then shook her head. "I didn't think so. You weren't wearing a locket when you came in, Rosie. We would have removed it when we took X-rays, but there's no record of it. Sorry."

"Maybe it fell off when you were dragged," Bess suggested. "Maybe we'll come across it if we search around the student union."

And if we find it, maybe the locket will lead us to Rosie's attacker, Nancy thought.

By the time the girls returned to campus, Nancy was eager to tour the student union.

Rosie's story about the attack had confirmed Fitz's version, and now Nancy wanted to check out the area where it had occurred.

It was nearly three when Nancy, Bess, and Kristin entered the lobby of the student union.

As they passed the bookstore, Kristin said, "I've got to work on my valentine for the auction. I've been procrastinating too long."

"I'd like to start mine, too," Bess said. "I saw some supplies this morning that would be absolutely perfect." She turned to Nancy and asked, "Do you mind if we leave you on your own for the tour of the building?"

"No problem," Nancy said. "Go work on your valentines. I'll meet you back at the Theta Pi house."

As the two girls disappeared into the bookstore, Nancy turned toward the pit. There, two televisions blared, one tuned to a soap opera, the other to a news program. The sofas and chairs had been claimed by students who were studying, talking, or napping between classes.

Stepping down into the lounge, Nancy went toward a campus phone. She dialed the union office and spoke to Fitz.

"I'll be right up," Fitz said. Five minutes later he appeared, a wide smile on his face. "I just spoke to Rosie," he said. "She sounds a little down but was happy to see you guys. Too bad she didn't see who hit her."

Nancy nodded. "That's why I'm here. I've

visited Emerson before, so I'm familiar with the general layout of this building. What I'd really like is a behind-the-scenes tour."

"An inside look . . ." Fitz said thoughtfully. "Well, I wouldn't do this for just *anybody*. But since you're a friend of the Theta Pis, I can't say no."

"Thanks," Nancy said, studying Fitz as they went down the ramp that cut through the center of the building.

"The weirdest thing about the student union is that the main entrance is on the top floor," Fitz explained. "The architects designed it that way since the building sort of leans into the hill."

On the floor below the main entrance, Fitz took Nancy through the laundromat, the student bank, and an old-fashioned candy store filled with glass jars of hard candies, chocolates, and licorice.

"Some of the student organizations also have offices on this floor," Fitz explained. He showed Nancy the suite used by Emerson's newspaper staff and the large student government office.

"When you and Rosie came into the building last night, did you notice anyone else around?" Nancy asked.

"It was pretty empty," Fitz said. He thought for a moment, then snapped his fingers. "Wait a second! When I passed by the snack bar on my way down to the office I think I saw Tamara Carlson and her boyfriend."

"Really?" Nancy was intrigued. "Did you speak with her?"

"No way. She and Rosie can't stand each other."

So Tamara was near the scene of the crime, Nancy thought. That's why she'd apparently made up an alibi.

When they descended the ramp to the ground floor, Nancy's senses were on alert. If Rosie had been dragged to the garden behind the union, it was likely that her attacker had taken her this way.

Fitz walked her through the large banquet room that was used for parties and dances. "This is where the Sweetheart Ball will be held on Saturday," he explained.

Two meeting rooms, each with a large conference table and more than a dozen chairs, and a kitchen were connected to the banquet hall. After walking through them, they returned to the bottom of the ramp.

"When I came down here, I went into the night manager's office, right there," Fitz said, leading Nancy to a narrow corridor on the far side of the ramp. It was lined with four doors. At the end of the hall, Nancy noticed a metal door.

Just then one of the doors along the hall opened, and a young woman peeked out and smiled. "Fitz! I was just going to page you on the intercom. You've got a call on line three."

"I'll be right back," he told Nancy, then followed the woman into the union office.

Glad for the time alone, Nancy looked at the metal door. This could be the way Rosie's attacker had left the building. It didn't seem likely to Nancy that whoever it was would have dragged her all the way around outside.

She spun around, trying to figure out which side of the building the garden backed up to. Following the hall to its end, she pushed open the metal door and peered inside.

The wide, short corridor beyond had an unfinished look, with a cement floor and two battered doors leading off it. The first one connected to a loading dock large enough to accommodate two trucks. Although it was now deserted, Nancy guessed that it was used to bring in food and supplies.

A second door led to a dark, windowless room where a huge, square furnace rumbled. Stepping inside, Nancy knew she'd hit pay dirt. The floor of the boiler room was smeared with a black soot thrown off by the furnace. As her eyes adjusted to the darkness, she could see the rectangular shape of a door on the opposite wall. She'd be willing to bet that door opened to the garden.

Rosie must have been dragged through this room after the attack!

On her right, Nancy noticed a workbench built into the cinder block wall. Careful not to touch anything, she looked over the wrenches and tools hanging on the wall and strewn on the countertop. Among the clutter she found a roll of electrical tape. That alone was not surprising. But when she came to an operating manual for the furnace, she quickly leafed through it and gasped. Part of one page had been torn out! The note pinned to Rosie's coat had been written on a scrap of paper torn from this booklet.

Had Rosie been attacked by someone on the staff of the building?

Just then the room seemed to shake as the furnace roared to life. Time to get out of here, Nancy thought. She needed to tell Dean Jarvis about her discoveries.

Nancy was about to turn away from the workbench when something caught her eye. Glimmering in the light of the furnace was a large wrench. Nancy was able to make out two strands of brown hair stuck to its rounded head. Was this the weapon used on Rosie?

Suddenly a beefy hand closed over her wrist, and Nancy let out a shriek. She spun around and found herself pinned to the worktable by a big man with smoldering eyes.

Chapter

Six

STUNNED, NANCY TRIED to step aside, but the large man held her arms back in a tight grasp. "Not so fast!"

Nancy's heart pounded madly as she stared into the man's grim, piercing eyes. The smell of sweat and soot threatened to overpower her as she tried to make out his face. The light from the furnace gave the angles of his jaw a hard look. Was this the man who had attacked Rosie?

"What're you doing in here?"

Fighting to appear calm, Nancy answered, "I was just touring the building—with Fitz. I guess I went through the wrong door."

"This place is off-limits to students," the man growled, releasing her arms at last.

Just then the door opened behind him, and

Fitz appeared, silhouetted in the light from the hallway. "Nancy? Max, what's going on?"

Max pointed at Nancy. "I came in to check the gauges on the furnace, and I found this girl wandering around. Keep your girlfriends out of my boiler room," he ordered, then pushed past Fitz into the hallway.

"Wait a second, Max! She's not my girl—" But the man didn't stop or slow down.

"Who is he?" Nancy asked.

"Max Dombrowski. He's on the maintenance staff, and among other things he takes care of the boiler," Fitz answered, turning back to Nancy. "He sure was in a rotten mood."

"Probably because I found some evidence that might implicate him as Rosie's attacker," Nancy said, glancing back at the workbench.

"Max? No way!" Fitz shook his head.

"Was he on duty last night?" she asked.

"Yeah, though I don't remember seeing him around," Fitz said. "But what kind of evidence did you find?"

Nancy showed him the tape and furnace manual, then pointed to the door. "Where does that exit lead?" she asked.

"To the garden. But it's locked from the outside," Fitz explained. "Is that important?"

"Absolutely," Nancy said. "In fact, if you show me the nearest phone, I'll call Dean Jarvis. He'll probably want to check out this room."

Within minutes the dean arrived at the student union. He was joined by Sergeant Weinberg and another officer from the local police, who brought a forensic kit to collect evidence.

Fitz seemed surprised that a wrench and a furnace manual could stir up so much interest. After the investigators arrived, he was called out to the loading docks to oversee a delivery.

Nancy watched as the officers put the wrench, tape, and booklet in plastic bags. "We'll confirm that they match our other evidence and check them for prints," Sergeant Weinberg explained. "But all in all, it looks like the victim was brought into this room."

With high-powered flashlights, they searched the soot-covered floor and discovered tracks leading out the door. After they photographed the drag marks, Nancy followed the officers through the steel door leading to the garden. She circled the stone fountain.

The day was overcast and dry, but there was certainly more light than there had been at night.

"When I visited Rosie at the hospital, she discovered that her Sweetheart locket was missing," Nancy told the police. She described the locket, but after a half hour of searching the frozen grass, no one had come across the gold necklace.

As the police continued to search the area, Nancy and the dean discussed the investigation.

"Rosie didn't see who attacked her," Nancy

told him, "but she thinks it was Tamara Carlson. And Fitz recalls seeing Tamara and her boyfriend in this building late last night."

"Tamara Carlson, the girl who'll be Sweetheart now that Rosie's been eliminated," Dean Jarvis said thoughtfully.

"Do you know her?" Nancy asked. "Do you think she's capable of attacking Rosie?"

Dean Jarvis sighed. "The rivalry between Rosie and Tamara was brought to my attention after an unfortunate incident last spring. They were involved in an altercation during Songfest."

After what Mindy had told her, Nancy wasn't surprised. "Why did they argue?"

Dean Jarvis shook his head as if it pained him to recall the incident. "Tamara Carlson was elected Songfest queen, and Rosie came in second. Traditionally, the girls in the queen's court all wear matching dresses, but Rosie didn't like the style Tamara chose. When Rosie showed up in a different dress, the girls got into a screaming match. Apparently, Tamara tore Rosie's gown."

Nancy frowned.

"I gave both students reprimands," said the dean. "We can't allow that kind of behavior."

"Rosie never mentioned it," Nancy said.

"I'm sure she'd rather forget it," Dean Jarvis replied. "But when it comes to competing against each other, there's no telling what those two are capable of."

"Then there's Max Dombrowski," Nancy said, telling the dean about her frightening encounter with the maintenance man. "It looks like Rosie was attacked with one of Max's tools. And Fitz says that Max was on duty last night—though I don't know what would have motivated him to harm a student."

Dean Jarvis frowned. "We have a large staff, and I'm afraid I don't know Max very well. But I'll check his employment file."

By the time the police had finished searching the area, it was nearly five o'clock. Dinner was at six, and Ned was picking Nancy up at seven-thirty for the Sweetheart Feature.

How am I ever going to sit through a movie when this case is heating up? Nancy wondered as she hurried back to the Theta Pi house.

When Nancy opened the door of the house, she was shocked to find Casey Thompson squaring off with Fitz. It appeared that a fight was just about to break out.

"Casey?" Nancy asked, "What's going on?"

Juanita and Kristin looked on from the living room, alarmed.

"Casey was just leaving," Fitz said, putting his hands on his hips so that his chest expanded.

"I came over to return Rosie's ten-speed," Casey explained. "She left it at my dorm after we went on a bike trip. I didn't realize I'd be greeted by a lynch mob."

"Why don't you just go before somebody gets hurt?" Fitz threatened.

"Easy, guys," Nancy said, surprised at Fitz's angry tone. She slipped her hand on Casey's shoulder and guided him toward the door. "I visited Rosie today," she told him quietly. "She seems to be doing okay."

"That's a relief." Casey gripped the doorknob. "Did she ask about me?"

"She said that she doesn't think you were the one who attacked her," Nancy answered.

"That's some consolation," Casey said, stepping out the door. "Now all I have to do is get the rest of the campus to believe I'm innocent." With that, he made a quick exit.

"He's got some nerve," Juanita said when he'd gone. "Coming around here after what he did to Rosie."

"Juanita, I think you're overreacting," Brook said, emerging from the den. Nancy could see a group of girls working on their valentines in front of the television set. Bess stood in the doorway, listening curiously.

"There's no proof that Casey Thompson attacked Rosie," Nancy pointed out. She told them about the evidence the police had found in the boiler room. "Could Casey even gain access to that room?" Nancy asked Fitz.

He shrugged. *"You* did," he pointed out. "The boiler room is supposed to be locked, but sometimes Max is careless."

"Well, whether or not he attacked Rosie, Casey Thompson is no friend of mine," Juanita said. "It's a good thing Fitz was here to help him carry that bike down to the basement. *I* wouldn't have gone down there alone with him."

"Let's not forget about Tamara Carlson," Kristin pointed out. "We just got a call from Rosie. She definitely won't be out of the hospital before the weekend. So Tamara's the new Sweetheart."

"And Fitz saw Tamara and her boyfriend in the student union last night," Nancy said.

"And it was just minutes before Rosie was attacked," Fitz added tensely.

A silence fell as everyone wondered who the attacker could be. "I don't know who to blame anymore," Kristin said.

"Hey, girls," called a voice from the kitchen. Trish appeared in the doorway, wearing a striped apron. "The spaghetti sauce is simmering, but we need help with the salad. Any volunteers?"

"I'll do it," Nancy said, glad for the diversion.

"Me, too," said Bess.

"Me, three!" Fitz chimed in.

The other girls went back into the den, and Trish led the new recruits into the kitchen.

"Hi, guys!" Mindy called. She was standing at a counter spooning melted butter on a long loaf of Italian bread sliced lengthwise. "I'm making garlic bread."

"I'm working on the sauce," Trish said.

Nancy peeked into a huge simmering pot of sauce as she tied on an apron.

"Just point me to the lettuce," Bess offered.

"And I'll just be the lovable kitchen pest," Fitz joked, perching on the counter near Mindy and sticking a strand of dry linguine into his mouth.

"So what else is new?" Mindy teased.

"Be kind, or I won't bid on your valentine, young lady," Fitz told her.

"Hah!" Mindy laughed. "I heard a rumor that you're going to the ball with Kristin."

Fitz shrugged. "So sue me. Doesn't mean I can't drive up the bidding on a few other valentines. What's yours going to be, Nancy?"

"I haven't thought about it much," Nancy admitted. "I've been too busy tracking down Rosie's attacker."

"When Nancy gets a case, she really throws herself into it," Bess explained.

"I saw that firsthand this afternoon," Fitz said. "By the way, did the police come up with any new theories?"

"They're convinced that Rosie was dragged through the boiler room," Nancy said as she tore lettuce. "And I found the weapon—a wrench."

"Wow," Bess said, slicing a carrot into thin strips. "And what about the maintenance man you mentioned—Max? Do you think he attacked Rosie?"

"I don't know," Nancy said.

"A new suspect appears every time you turn

around," Mindy said. "Casey, Tamara—now Max."

"It's hard to keep up, even for a gossip hound like you," Fitz said lightly, punching Mindy on the arm.

"Cut it out," she said, sidestepping him and knocking over a box of pasta. A shower of spaghetti spilled out, bouncing onto the floor.

Mindy winced. "Oops!"

"Nice move," Trish said. "You'll have to get the broom. It's in the basement."

"I'm up to my wrists in garlic butter," Mindy said.

"I'll get it," Nancy said, wiping her hands on her apron.

The basement door was beside the refrigerator. Nancy opened it, stepped onto the landing, and turned toward the steps on the left. The stairs were dark. She ran her left hand along the wall, feeling for the light switch.

Her hand closed around something—and suddenly her heart seemed to lurch out of her chest as an electric current shot up her arm!

Chapter

Seven

NANCY REELED BACKWARD and fell onto the threshold of the door. Everything went black for a second as her heart hammered wildly. She covered her face with her hands, still feeling stunned by the shock.

"What happened?" Bess called.

"She's hurt!" Fitz exclaimed as everyone rushed over and gathered around Nancy. They pulled her to her feet and helped her into one of the vinyl kitchen chairs.

"Nan, you look pale as a ghost," Bess said, rubbing Nancy's back. "What happened?"

"I got a shock," Nancy told them, starting to feel better at last. "I was reaching for the light switch, but the wires are exposed."

"*What?*" Mindy's mouth dropped open in disbelief.

"How could that be?" Trish asked.

"I don't get it," Fitz said. "Casey and I were just down there with Rosie's bike. We would have noticed it."

"Wait a second," Mindy said, touching Fitz's shoulder. "Do you think that Casey could have set it up—like a trap—while you weren't looking?" Her dark eyes filled with horror at the thought.

"Is there another way into the basement?" Nancy asked the girls.

Kristin nodded. "There's a door from the basement to the backyard, but it's kept locked."

"Let's go down and see if it's locked now," Nancy said.

With the help of a flashlight from the kitchen drawer, Nancy and Fitz checked out the light switch. The switch plate had been removed, and a wire dangled from the mechanism inside.

"It's definitely been tampered with," Fitz commented.

The two of them descended the stairs and carefully made their way through the dark, musty basement until they reached the back door. Nancy pulled the knob, but the door didn't budge. "It's bolted tight," she said. "Whoever rigged that switch must have come in through the upstairs."

When Nancy and Fitz returned to the kitchen, it was crowded with Theta Pi sisters.

"This is unbelievable!" Fitz said.

"The question is," Bess said, "could Casey have rigged the switch this afternoon?"

"Let me think," Fitz said. "I kept an eye on him . . . but then I started rearranging some boxes to make room for the bike. He was already in the kitchen by the time I came back up."

"And do you remember turning the basement light off?" Nancy asked.

"Not really. I'm not even sure we turned it on when we went down. It was still pretty light." He shook his head. "The switch could have been rigged then. I'd say Casey's your man."

"This is getting really weird," Trish said.

"That's for sure." Denise folded her arms as she looked from one sister to another. "Casey's not going to stop with Rosie. He's out to hurt all of us!"

Bess frowned. "He thinks Rosie broke up with him because of Theta Pi."

Everyone started talking at once as panic set in. Nancy understood their fear, but she wanted them to realize that there were other suspects.

"Wait a second!" Nancy held up her hands until the group quieted down. "We've got no proof that Casey's the culprit. But one thing is sure. Someone's out to hurt the Theta Pis. You should all be on guard."

The girls listened intently as Nancy added, "But you should also realize that Casey wasn't the only one with access to that light switch." She cast a pointed look at Fitz, but no one seemed to pick up on it.

"We're all targets now," Kristin said somberly. "This is the real test of sisterhood. We've got to watch out for each other."

The girls voiced their agreement and promised to stay alert and cautious. As they began to file out of the kitchen and set the dining room table for dinner, Nancy took Fitz aside.

"Let's talk in the den, where there's less commotion," she said, leading the way.

The small, cozy den was empty. Fitz flopped down on an overstuffed couch and sighed. "What a day! First Rosie, and now this."

Nancy nodded. "And the more I investigate, the murkier this case seems to get. I thought you might be able to help me think some of the details through, since you were nearby when Rosie was attacked *and* when that light switch was rigged."

Nancy studied his face for a reaction, but Fitz seemed guiltless as he tossed a small pillow in the air, then pushed back his dark bangs.

"Boy, I wish I could help you," he said. "I'd love to nail the guy who did this stuff."

"Guy?" Nancy repeated.

"Just a guess," Fitz said, shrugging. "But if Casey isn't the culprit, I'm afraid it could be our maintenance man, Max." He buried his face in his hands for a moment, then frowned up at

Nancy. "I hate to point the finger at a guy on staff, but when I think of the wrench and the other stuff you found today . . . well, it seems pretty obvious."

"Why do you think Max is Cupid?" Nancy asked. "Is he connected to the sorority in any way?"

Fitz's face reddened. "Why're you asking me?"

"Only because you're so involved with the girls in this house," Nancy said pointedly.

"I don't know what makes Max tick," Fitz said. "But for me, being friends with the Theta Pis is the best thing I've got going here at Emerson. Maybe it's because my older sister died last year. Jessie and I were really close. I like thinking that I have a lot of sisters, right here in this house."

As he spoke, Nancy felt sorry for Fitz. Granted it was a little strange that he spent so much time with the girls and didn't seem to have any male friends. But there was something endearing about the guy. And it was awfully sad about his sister.

"Just do me a favor and remind the Theta Pis to be extra cautious until Cupid is caught," she said. "They trust you, and they'll listen to you."

"Will do," Fitz agreed, a grin spreading across his face.

"The Sweetheart Feature starts in twenty minutes!" Kristin called up the stairs of the sorority house. The sisters who didn't have dates were attending the film as a group so that no one would be left in the house alone.

Ned had already arrived and was standing in the front hall. "Ready for *Hearts Aflame?*" he asked, winking at Nancy as she came downstairs. "It's a 1950s classic."

"How romantic," Bess said, putting on her jacket. "Hey," she told Nancy and Ned, "why don't you two go on ahead? I'll stick with the Theta Pis so you can pretend you're on a date."

"Okay." Nancy laughed as she pulled on her mittens. "We'll see you later."

The film was being shown in the theater that was also used for plays and assemblies. The main entrance of the Gothic-style building was decorated with red and white streamers and red balloons that fluttered in the steady wind.

Nancy laughed when she saw the candy displayed at the refreshment stand—red cinnamon hearts, red licorice, and solid chocolate hearts. "They're really into Valentine's Day," she said as Ned bought a box of chocolate hearts.

As they walked down the theater aisle looking for a seat, Nancy spotted Tamara Carlson snuggled up to a handsome guy wearing a red-and-white Russell University letter jacket. That's Tamara's boyfriend, Nancy recalled. Zip Williams had been a suspect in a case she'd investigated at Emerson. In the end, she had proved that he was innocent.

Nancy smiled at the couple sitting on the aisle, but the minute Tamara spotted Nancy, her face scrunched up in anger, and she jumped out of her seat. "Just a second, Nancy—" she called.

Ned looked on in surprise as Tamara marched up to them and snapped at Nancy, "Have you got a problem?"

"Excuse me?" Nancy said.

"I know what you've been saying." Tamara's dark eyes flashed. "The word's out on campus that you've got me on your list. You think I knocked out Rosie? Well, think again. I didn't touch her. So why don't you back off?"

"Easy, now," Ned said.

"I'm trying to find out what really happened," Nancy said. "And you've already lied to me, Tamara. You didn't go back to the Delta House after last night's game. You were seen in the student union—near the scene of the crime."

Tamara's nostrils flared. "So?" she hissed. "That doesn't prove anything."

"We'll have proof soon enough," Nancy said, studying Tamara's face for a reaction. "The police found the weapon. They're analyzing it for fingerprints right now."

"Big deal." Tamara rolled her eyes. "Leave it to Rosie to launch a police investigation."

She doesn't seem at all concerned about being caught, Nancy thought. Maybe Tamara wasn't involved in the attack. "Why did you lie if you have nothing to hide?" Nancy probed.

Tamara pouted as she considered the question, then she waved Nancy off. "Forget it. I'm not letting Rosie Lopez drag me into more trouble. Just keep me out of this!" She spun on her heel and walked back to her seat.

"There goes one unhappy suspect," Ned said as he and Nancy continued down the aisle. They passed Mindy and Fitz, who were sitting together at the end of one row. In front of them, a handful of Theta Pis sat with Bess. Nancy and Ned found seats off to the side, away from the crowd.

"This case is getting weirder by the minute," Nancy said as Ned slipped his arm around her shoulders. She told him about how she'd been shocked by the rigged light switch.

"Nancy!" Gently, he smoothed a hand over her reddish gold hair. "You could have been hurt! You'd better be careful."

"All the girls are on the alert now," she promised. "But I'm beginning to feel that I'm walking on eggshells. One wrong step and everything could crack." She sighed. "I've got to solve this case before Cupid strikes again."

"You'll figure it out," Ned said as the lights dimmed and the movie started.

At first Nancy found it hard to focus on the film because thoughts of the case kept whirling through her mind. But when the hero began to remind her of Ned, she got hooked on the movie.

Hearts Aflame told the story of two researchers separated when the South American rain forest where they were conducting a study was ravaged by fire. The two characters traveled the world, continuing their research, never sure if the other one was still alive. Nancy found herself crying when the two of them found each other at last.

As the movie ended, Ned gave her a hug. "I'm a sucker for a good romance," he said.

"You're a soft touch, Nickerson," Nancy said. "But that's why I love you."

They filed down the aisle. Outside it was snowing. "Snow. I love it," Nancy said delightedly, linking her arm through Ned's.

"Looks like an inch already, and the weather service predicted a few more," he said, pausing to zip his jacket.

While Ned was distracted, Nancy crept behind him and scooped up a handful of snow. "Hey, Nickerson," she called. "Think fast!"

Ned turned around just in time to catch a snowball in the shoulder. "Cheap shot!" he protested, scrambling to scrape up a patch of snow. "But I've got a killer hook shot!"

Nancy laughed when the snowball hit her arm. "Two points!" she cried as she packed another one.

As other moviegoers streamed past, Nancy and Ned enticed a few to join in the fight, and soon snowballs were flying through the air.

By the time the battle wound down, Nancy had nearly forgotten the trouble at the sorority house earlier. But as she and Ned turned up the walkway to the Theta Pi house, Nancy noticed that a group of sisters were gathered in the driveway, pointing to the back of the house.

"Looks like trouble," Ned said as they quickened their pace.

"What's going on?" Nancy called out. "Is everyone okay?"

"No one's been hurt," Brook answered. "But our house has been vandalized."

"It must have happened while we were all at the Sweetheart Feature," said Kristin.

Pushing through the crowd, Nancy hurried to assess the damage.

Graffiti had been scrawled across the white siding on the back of the house. Nancy read the message splashed in green paint:

THETA PI MUST DIE!

It was signed "CUPID."

Chapter

Eight

This is no joke," Mindy said, staring at the message. "Someone's definitely out to get us."

Nancy studied the graffiti. Despite the dripping paint, she could see that the letters were scrawled in the same block print used in the note that had been pinned to Rosie's coat. At least Cupid was consistent.

Ned scowled. "This Cupid is a real creep."

"We need to notify campus security," Nancy said, realizing that Dean Jarvis would want to know about this and the rigged electrical switch.

"I'll make the call," Kristin offered.

"Let me go with you," Nancy said, following the girl into the house. After Kristin notified security, the campus operator put Nancy through to Dean Jarvis's home. She gave him a quick rundown on the two incidents, and they agreed to meet in his office the next morning.

"In the meantime, I'll alert campus security to keep a close watch on the Theta Pi house," he said. "It seems that Cupid is acting out a vendetta against the sorority."

Outside, Nancy found Ned helping a few of the girls clean off the excess wet paint. "You'll be able to paint over it tomorrow after this has dried," he told them. "But it'll take a few coats of white to cover this green."

The girls thanked Ned, then filed into the house through the kitchen door. "Will you please tell them to be careful?" Ned whispered to Nancy as he paused just inside the kitchen door.

"They've already been warned," Nancy said. "Thanks for a fun night—till now, at least."

Ned shrugged. "I've got to spend the morning hitting the books for a psych test. What are you going to do?"

"I need to have a talk with Tamara's boyfriend, Zip Williams," Nancy said.

"But he's over at Russell U," Ned said.

"It's only a few miles away," Nancy replied. "And I've got to find out the inside story on Tamara. Besides, he owes me a favor."

"I'll catch up with you in the afternoon." Ned dropped a kiss on her cheek, then backed out the door.

Upstairs in their bedroom, the girls discussed

the recent turn of events as they got ready for bed.

"It gives me the jitters to think someone's out to get us," Kristin said, crawling under her comforter.

"And did you notice the color of the paint? Green," Mindy said as she brushed out her shiny black hair. "That's Delta Zeta's color."

"Do you think Tamara painted the graffiti?" Bess asked as she buttoned her nightgown.

Nancy shook her head. "I don't think she's the person we're looking for. First of all, I don't think she could sneak into the basement of this house to rig a switch without attracting attention. And as far as the graffiti goes, I saw her in the theater before the movie began."

"I did, too," Kristin said. "She was with her boyfriend, Zip Williams. I saw them as they were leaving the theater after the movie. So you're right, Nancy. Tamara couldn't have painted that message."

Mindy frowned. "I didn't notice them. But isn't it strange that the message was painted in one of Delta's colors?"

"Maybe someone would like us to believe that Delta Zeta is behind the vandalism," Nancy said. "But let's think about other suspects. Who *wasn't* at the film when the graffiti was painted?"

The girls were silent for a moment as they

considered the question. Then, in unison, they answered, "Casey Thompson!"

"The whole world is covered with white stuff!" Fitz said as he peered into the kitchen on Thursday morning.

"Good morning, Fitz," Kristin said, smiling up at him. His black hair was sprinkled with snowflakes.

Nancy, Bess, Kristin, and Brook were sitting at the kitchen table, finishing off bowls of oatmeal with brown sugar and cream. They had been staring out the window, watching the snow. It was coming down heavily, and the backyard was buried under mounds of snow.

"I come bearing gifts." Fitz held up an electrical switch plate and a large heart-shaped box of candy.

"That's beautiful!" Brook said, taking the pink-and-red box from him. Beneath the clear plastic wrap, the box was decorated with satin ribbon and a spray of tiny plastic hearts. "Who's it for? All of us?"

"It must be for me," Kristin teased, looking over Brook's shoulder.

"Check the card," Fitz said as he opened the door to the basement and assessed the job ahead of him.

A white envelope was taped to the plastic. "No name on it," Brook said as she ripped it open and pulled out a Valentine's Day greeting card. "It says 'Your secret admirer,'" Brook said. "Is this from you, Fitz?"

"I found it sitting out on the front porch," he explained, sliding his black leather knapsack to the floor and shaking the snow off his coat.

"A secret admirer," Bess said dreamily. "Who could it be for?"

Brook and Kristin smiled at each other.

"I don't know," Brook said, "but I have a feeling every girl in this sorority is going to claim this package."

They all laughed.

"Considering what's been going on around here, maybe you should make sure the candy came from someone you trust," Nancy pointed out.

Brook examined the heart-shaped box. "But it's sealed in plastic. And it would be a shame to waste such a huge box of chocolates."

Kristin nodded. "Let's save it for the rush tea this afternoon. We can serve the candy then, and everyone will get a kick out of the secret admirer story."

"A rush tea?" Bess said curiously.

"It's a chance for sisters and potential pledges to get acquainted," Kristin explained. "They get to learn about our sorority, and we check them out to see if they'd fit in. After we get through a series of rush events, we'll choose the girls we'd like to join the sorority and begin pledging them."

"I'm the rush chairperson," Brook added, checking her watch. "Which reminds me—I have classes all morning, and we need some snacks for the tea at three." She pulled a grocery list off the refrigerator door and handed it to Kristin. "Can you make a run into town?"

"I guess I can squeeze it in around lunchtime," she said, eyeing the list. "But I have to get out of here, or I'll be late for an economics quiz."

"And we've got a few leads to check out," Nancy said, nodding at Bess. "Though this snow has put a crimp in my original plan."

"Do you really think Tamara's boyfriend will talk to you?" Bess asked.

"I have to try," Nancy said. "Rosie is convinced that she's the one who attacked her. Even Dean Jarvis said that the girls were reprimanded for fighting. Tamara may have been at the Sweetheart Feature when the graffiti artist struck, but I need to find out what she was really doing on Tuesday night."

After the house emptied out, Nancy went to the secluded nook at the top of the stairs and picked up the phone. With so much snow on the ground, she knew it wouldn't be wise to drive to Russell University. Instead, she dialed the number of the school's switchboard and asked for Zip Williams. The operator put her through.

"Hello?" a deep voice answered.

"Zip? This is Nancy Drew."

Zip's response was cool. "I know what you're calling about," he told her. "You're snooping around about Tamara."

"I'm trying to clear her," Nancy said. "I don't think she's responsible for the attack on Rosie Lopez, but her alibi doesn't check out."

"You won't give up until you figure this thing out, will you?" he said, sighing. "Okay, okay. The truth is, Tamara and I went over to the student union snack bar after the game. She was hungry, but she didn't want to stick around in the gym and watch Rosie gloat. So after we had some burgers, I walked Tamara back to the Delta house and said good night. That's all, and it's the truth."

"Why did she lie to me?" Nancy asked, wrapping the telephone cord around her finger.

Zip remained silent for a moment. Then he cleared his throat and said, "She's nervous about having been so close to the place where Rosie was attacked. But after the way you cleared my name, I figure you should know the truth."

"Thanks, Zip." Nancy smiled as she hung up. One suspect down—and a few more to go, she thought.

Minutes later, Nancy and Bess were making their way across the bright white campus. Most of the paths had been cleared and salted, and as they headed toward Dean Jarvis's office, Nancy recapped her conversation with Tamara's boyfriend.

"So that rules Tamara out," she concluded. "She didn't hurt Rosie. And she couldn't have painted that graffiti."

"Then that narrows the suspects down to Casey Thompson and Max Dombrowski," Bess said.

Nancy remained silent as they entered the administration building.

She and Bess didn't have to wait long to speak with Dean Jarvis. After the girls had taken seats in his office, Nancy told him what she'd learned about Tamara Carlson. "She isn't the person behind these incidents," she said, explaining what Zip had said.

"That's good to hear," he said, "especially since Tamara is now Sweetheart. But I'm concerned about these attacks on the Theta Pi sisters."

"It looks like a vendetta," Nancy said.

He nodded as he leafed through a file on his desk. "Sergeant Weinberg called me this morning. The police lab found traces of Rosie's hair and blood on that wrench from the boiler room. The electrical tape and manual also matched— though they couldn't get any clean fingerprints."

"What about Max Dombrowski?" Nancy asked.

"I've checked the time sheets from Tuesday night, and he was on duty," the dean said. "In fact, his file shows that he was trained as an electrician."

"It really sounds like Max is the culprit," Nancy said. "I don't know what his motive was, but all the evidence points to him."

Dean Jarvis lifted his glasses. "But he was working in the sports complex from nine o'clock on. I spoke with a campus security guard who remembers seeing him there."

"Was he there all night?" Nancy pressed.

"I don't know. But I can't accuse Max. His employee record is clean. And he's a family man with a wife and two daughters, one of whom attends Emerson."

A daughter at Emerson? Nancy's thoughts were spinning. "Is his daughter in a sorority?" Nancy asked the dean. Maybe she's a Delta Zeta sister, she thought, recalling the graffiti that had been painted in one of Delta's colors.

"Let's see," he said, turning to the computer beside his desk. He punched in some information and waited as a file appeared on the monitor. "Her name is Marina Dombrowski . . . and no, she has not pledged a sorority."

"Hmmm." Nancy frowned. "I'm not sure what his motive could be. Can you call him in? Maybe he'll confess if we put a little pressure on him?"

Dean Jarvis shook his head. "Much as I admire your investigative skills, I can't let you interrogate a campus employee in this office."

Nancy glanced away from the older man. Maybe she had pushed a little too hard.

"But I'll call him in and speak to him," the dean said.

"Fair enough," Nancy replied, her mind already racing on to the other suspects. If Max didn't have anything to do with the attack, that left Casey Thompson—and then there was Fitz.

"Can you check Mike Fitzgerald's file?" Nancy asked. "He was the last guy seen with Rosie, and he works in the student union. He has keys to the whole building."

"Fitz?" Bess's blue eyes widened. "But he's such a nice guy! And the Theta Pis love him. Besides, he was sitting next to Mindy at the movie. He couldn't have painted the graffiti."

"His record is impeccable," Dean Jarvis added, reading the computer screen. "He's premed, with a high grade point average. Has a part-time job on campus."

"And he obviously cares a lot about the girls in the sorority," Nancy said, tapping a nail on the top of the dean's desk. Casey seemed more and more likely, though she still couldn't help but wonder about Max. At any rate, she had to catch Cupid—before he struck again!

* * *

As Nancy and Bess walked up the driveway of the Theta Pi house, Kristin was scraping snow off the windows of her car.

"This is going to be an adventure," Kristin told Nancy and Bess. "I've got to get snacks for rush, but I don't know whether or not the Emersonville roads have been plowed yet."

"Maybe we should go along," Bess suggested as she wiped a mound of snow off the car's bumper. "If you get stuck in the snow, there'll be two extra people to shovel and push."

"Good idea," Nancy agreed. The three girls cleared a path out of the driveway. Then they piled into the car.

Kristin drove slowly. "So far so good," she said as she turned onto the road leading down the hill to the main part of town. The street had been cleared, so Kristin drove a little faster.

As the road dipped, the car picked up speed, and Kristin applied the brakes.

"Easy," Nancy said as the car skidded.

Kristin tightened her grip on the wheel. "It's weird, but we're sliding—a lot!"

"The road doesn't seem that icy," Nancy said. "Try pumping the brakes."

"It's not working!" Kristin cried, stepping on the brake pedal frantically as the car careened ahead. "The brakes—they're not working!"

Nancy stared ahead. The car was speeding toward a treacherous curve in the road.

They were going to crash!

Chapter

Nine

WE'LL NEVER MAKE that turn up ahead!" Bess cried from the backseat.

Nancy knew that Kristin had to slow the car somehow, or they would go flying off the road and down the side of the hill. "Switch to low gear!" Nancy shouted.

Kristin grabbed the gear shift and shoved it into first. There was a jerking motion as the car slowed.

"That helped," Kristin bit out the words as she tried to steer into the skid. The nose of the car stayed on the curving road. But the rear end fishtailed, propelling the car toward the narrow shoulder on the side of the hilltop.

The car bounced out of the turn, and Kristin turned the wheel again, steering the car back onto the right side of the road. Her hands were riveted to the wheel.

The rest of the ride was rough, but there were no more hairpin turns to negotiate. At last they made it to the bottom of the hill, rolling to a stop a few blocks short of Main Street. Kristin pulled the car onto the shoulder and killed the engine.

"That was close!" Bess said.

"I don't understand it." Kristin rested her head on the steering wheel, then looked over at Nancy. "This car is old, but I take good care of it. The brakes were replaced last year."

Nancy frowned. "Why don't you open the hood and we'll take a look?"

Wind and snow whipped around them as the girls huddled at the front end of the car. Although Nancy wasn't a mechanical expert, she had had enough experience to know that the car had been tampered with.

"Here's the problem," she said, holding up a cable coated with plastic. "This cable was cut in half."

"Someone cut the brake lines?" Kristin said, her mouth dropping open in surprise.

"We could have been killed," Bess said, shaking her head. "That's another strike against Theta Pi."

"You're right," Nancy told Bess. "We'd better call the sorority house and warn the other girls to check their cars."

"And I'd better get this one to a mechanic," Kristin said, shielding her eyes against the snow. "There's a gas station a few blocks away. Maybe they can fix it."

Twenty minutes later the girls were sitting in the corner booth of a diner on Main Street. An attendant at the service station had sent over a tow truck to get Kristin's car. Nancy had phoned the Theta Pi house to warn the sisters. Then the three girls had walked over to the diner, where they could stay warm and eat some lunch.

"The mechanic said that you were right about the brake lines being cut. But he won't have my car fixed until tomorrow," Kristin said as a short, round waitress placed bowls of steaming clam chowder on the table.

"How're we going to get back to Emerson?" Bess asked. "Doesn't the Theta Pi rush begin at three?"

The waitress remained at the table. She was staring at Kristin. "I thought I recognized you," she said. "You're a Theta Pi, right?"

"She's the president of the sorority," Bess offered as she picked up her spoon. "And we're her friends, Bess Marvin and Nancy Drew."

"You look familiar, too," Kristin said, eyeing the waitress. "You're a student at Emerson, right?"

"A sophomore," the waitress said. "Did you guys get stuck in the snow?"

"Something like that," Nancy said cautiously.

With her square face and dark, curly hair the waitress seemed vaguely familiar to her, too, but she couldn't figure out why.

"My shift ends at two, and I'm headed back to school," the waitress said. "I'd be happy to give you a lift."

Kristin stared down at her soup, then smiled up at the girl. "We've got a few errands to take care of. It'll be easier if we call a taxi. But thanks for the offer. What's your name again?"

"Marina," the waitress said. "Marina Dombrowski." She smiled. Just then someone called her name from the kitchen. "Whoops! I think the rest of your order is ready. I'll be right back." She turned and disappeared into the kitchen.

"Is something wrong?" Bess asked Nancy.

"Marina Dombrowski," Nancy repeated. "No wonder she looks familiar! She's Max's daughter."

"The maintenance man from the student union!" Bess said, her eyes wide. "Dean Jarvis mentioned that he had a daughter."

"I didn't know that he was her father," Kristin said, glancing back at the kitchen to make sure Marina was out of earshot. "That's a weird connection, though. Marina wanted to pledge Theta Pi last year, but we didn't extend a bid, and she was really bitter about the whole thing."

"What's a bid?" Bess asked, as she carefully took a taste of the steaming chowder.

"An invitation to join the sorority. After a few weeks of 'rushing,' each sorority reviews the list of rushees and decides which ones to extend bids to. If a girl accepts a bid, she becomes a pledge. Pledges spend a few weeks learning about the sorority. It's kind of a trial period before initiation."

Nancy frowned thoughtfully. "So not every girl who rushes gets a bid, right?"

"Right," Kristin said. "Lots of sophomores who didn't receive bids as freshmen choose to rush again, and some of them are given bids the second time around." She lowered her voice. "The funny thing was, Marina threw a fit when she didn't get a bid from us. She told Denise, our rush chairperson last year, that we'd regret it."

"That's kind of creepy," Bess said.

Kristin nodded. "I know rejection is hard to take, but most girls are good sports about it."

Nancy was only half listening to Kristin's explanation. Max's daughter had been rejected by the sisters of Theta Pi! The man—and his daughter—had a motive for the crimes against the sorority. Maybe they were working together.

"This sheds a new light on Max as a suspect," Nancy said quietly. "We'll need to do some checking on Marina. And I still want to confirm Casey's whereabouts on Tuesday night."

Just then Marina emerged from the kitchen and brought their sandwiches to the table. They changed the subject to the charity auction.

"I still haven't come up with an angle for my valentine," Nancy said.

"Not me," Bess said. "I'm all set. As long as Kyle makes it to Emerson in time."

The girls tried to keep the conversation light as they ate, especially since Marina seemed to be hovering nearby. Afterward they paid the check and hurried off to the supermarket to pick up the items they needed.

While Bess and Kristin waited in line at the checkout counter, Nancy went across the street to the Video Zone, where Casey claimed to have spent the latter part of Tuesday night. The guy on the phone had told her to check back on Friday, but since she was nearby, she thought it was worth a shot.

"A friend of mine was here late Tuesday night," she told the guy on duty. "Is there anyone I can talk to who might have seen him?"

The guy looked around the quiet arcade and shrugged. "Not right now. You need to talk to Tiger." He gave her an aloof smile. "Are you the girl who called yesterday? Ha!" He laughed. "You must be really stuck on Tiger if you keep dreaming up bogus reasons to talk to him."

"I—" Nancy started to argue, then realized it was useless. This guy wasn't going to give up. "Yeah," she said dreamily. "I'm wild about Tiger." She pulled a notepad out of her shoulder bag and scribbled the number of the Theta Pi house on it. "Here," she said, handing the guy the slip of paper. "If Tiger happens to turn up before tomorrow, would you have him call me?"

He shrugged. "I'll give him the message, but there's no guarantee. Tiger's a popular guy."

"Thank goodness you're back!" Brook exclaimed as she greeted the girls at the front door of the Theta Pi house. She took the grocery bags from Nancy and Bess.

When Nancy had called the house, she hadn't given details. Now Brook gasped as Kristin described the near accident. "I guess Cupid's struck again." She shook her head. "I can't bear to even think about it now. The rushees will be arriving in fifteen minutes, and we specified tea attire. You'd better change."

"What about the coffee urn?" Kristin asked. "And the music? Did Etta pick up the flowers?"

"It's all under control, Madam President," Brook said. "Your sisters wouldn't let you down. But you'd better get cleaned up—unless you want to meet the rushees in your snowboots."

Nancy, Bess, and Kristin bounded up the stairs, peeling off their mittens and jackets along the way. They dashed into their bedroom, then stopped short when they noticed Mindy curled up in her bed.

"Hey, sleepyhead!" Kristin teased. "Up and at 'em! It's almost time for the rush."

"I feel lousy," Mindy said. She rolled over to face them, and Nancy could see that her face was flushed. "My stomach's rocky, and my head hurts. Maybe I'm coming down with the flu."

"That's a shame," Nancy said.

"Anything we can get you?" Bess asked.

Mindy shook her head. "No, thanks. But you'd better hurry, or you'll miss the greeting."

Bess was already taking a cherry-colored sweater and matching skirt out of the closet. "I didn't realize we'd be dressing up for this," she said. "Do you think this is okay?" she asked Mindy.

"Perfect," Mindy said, clutching her knees.

"Some of the rushes are informal," Kristin explained as she sat on the edge of her bed and tugged off her boots. "Today's just happens to be one of the fancier occasions."

Kristin finished changing first. Like a shot, she was out of the room and down the stairs. Not long after that, Bess had wound her blond hair into a sophisticated French twist.

"You look great," Nancy said as she pulled a gold-and-black brocade vest over her black wool dress. She followed Bess out the bedroom door. "That's got to be a record breaker for you, Bess. Completely transformed in less than ten minutes."

"I'm so glad to be included in a sorority rush. I don't want to miss a single second," Bess said as they hurried down the stairs.

When the doorbell rang, four of the sisters lined up at the foot of the stairs. As the front door was opened to the guests, the quartet sang a chorus of a Theta Pi song in four-part harmony. Other sisters took the rushees' coats and escorted them to the coffee and tea service in the dining room.

"Each rushee will get a carnation as she leaves, along with a booklet explaining the goals of Theta Pi," Kristin explained as Nancy and Bess looked on.

"Anything we can do to help?" Bess offered.

"With Mindy sick, we're a little light in the kitchen," Kristin said. "Do you mind?"

"No problem," Nancy said, turning toward the back of the house.

"Just make sure you're not stuck back there when I give my speech," Kristin called after them. "It's a real showstopper."

In the kitchen, Denise put Nancy to work filling sugar bowls and arranging tea packets in baskets. "And put these on here," she said, handing Bess the heart-shaped box of chocolates and a silver embossed tray.

"Someone's been sneaking some of the secret admirer's candy," Bess said as she removed the satin-covered lid from the box.

"That must have been Mindy," Denise said. "She's notorious for her sweet tooth."

Bess transferred some of the round chocolates to the platter, taking care not to dislodge them from their creased brown wrappers. She leaned close to the platter and sniffed. "They look like chocolate-covered cherries, but they smell like peanuts."

"Maybe they're assorted flavors," said Denise.

"We'll soon find out." Bess lifted the silver platter and ducked out of the kitchen.

Nancy tucked packets of raspberry tea into a basket, then paused. Something was nagging at her mind. The chocolates had an unusual odor . . . a few were missing . . . and Mindy was sick.

A handful of tea bags went flying as Nancy raced out of the kitchen. She pushed past Kristin and Etta, then skidded to a halt in the dining room. Beside the buffet, Bess stood, poised and charming, as she extended the platter to two guests.

"Change of plans," Nancy said, plucking a chocolate from one girl's hand. "We're going to save the best till last." Ignoring the girls' confused looks, she wheeled Bess around.

"Nancy?" Bess frowned. "What's going on?"

"You can't serve those chocolates," Nancy whispered, tugging Bess back toward the kitchen. "I think that candy's been poisoned!"

Chapter

Ten

"ARE YOU KIDDING?" Bess gasped as Nancy took the tray from her hands and strode into the kitchen.

"Did you serve the chocolates to anyone?" Nancy asked her.

"You caught me before I had a chance."

In the kitchen, Nancy dumped the chocolates back into the box and turned to Denise. "I think these chocolates were doctored. There's a rat poison called Rodenticide that smells like peanuts. Spread the word among the sisters and find out if anyone else has tried them."

"How awful!" Denise exclaimed. "I'll go tell Kristin and the others."

"What about Mindy?" Bess asked.

"If she ate this candy, I'm taking her straight to

the hospital," Nancy answered, tucking the box under her arm. "Let's go upstairs and check."

Nancy and Bess found Mindy curled up in bed, still feeling nauseated. "Did you eat any of the candy from the 'secret admirer'?" Nancy asked her.

Mindy nodded, "Just a few pieces. Not enough to give me a stomachache."

"I'll bet you anything I'm right," Nancy said, pulling their coats out of the closet. "Someone tampered with those chocolates! We'd better get you to a doctor fast."

While Kristin gave her speech to all the guests in the dining room, Nancy and Bess quietly helped Mindy down the stairs and outside.

Denise followed them to the porch, her breath forming a puff as she spoke. "None of the other sisters tried the candy."

"Thank goodness!" Bess said.

"We'll call you from the hospital," Nancy told Denise. They climbed into the Mustang, and Nancy drove straight to the Emersonville hospital. Fortunately the roads had been cleared, and Nancy was able to drive quickly.

Mindy was checked into the emergency room, and a nurse wheeled her inside for an examination.

"We think it was this candy that made her sick," Nancy said to the attending physician, placing the heart-shaped box of chocolates on the counter at the nurses' station. She opened the box and examined a few of the candies. There was no sign that any of them had been glazed or broken. But she knew that a poison could have been injected with a needle, leaving only the tiniest of holes.

As Nancy went on to explain about the problems that had been occurring at the Theta Pi house, the attending physician lowered his clipboard and listened closely. He was a young, soft-spoken man with brown, curly hair and a neatly trimmed mustache.

"We'll need to get a sample of this candy to the lab immediately," he told a nurse.

"Right away, Dr. Feldman," the nurse said.

"And you should notify Sergeant Weinberg at the police station," Nancy added. "If this candy was poisoned, he'll want to investigate."

After Dr. Feldman went inside to attend to Mindy, Nancy and Bess settled into chairs in the waiting room. For what seemed like an eternity, they waited, their eyes glued to the examining room door.

"I just wish we knew she was okay," Bess said, as she got up and paced back and forth.

Bess went to a pay phone to call the sorority house. Nancy noticed that Sergeant Weinberg had arrived and was speaking to a nurse at the reception desk. Nancy joined them, filling in the officer on her suspicions.

"When I realized that the candy smelled like

peanuts, I remembered reading about a rat poison with that distinctive odor. It's called Rodenticide," she explained. "Since Mindy was the only one who ate the chocolates, and she wasn't feeling well, it seemed likely that the candy had been tampered with."

The nurse said she would give the name of the rat poison to the attending physician and the lab.

"Your suspicions were correct," the doctor said a few minutes later as he entered the reception area. "We've treated Mindy for poisoning. She's going to be fine, but we're admitting her for observation. The nurses are trying to work it out so that she can share a room with her friend, Rosie Lopez."

"Thank goodness she's all right," Nancy said, taking a deep breath.

"Have you determined the source of the poison yet?" the sergeant asked.

"We believe it's the candy, although the lab hasn't had time to identify the toxic substance yet," Dr. Feldman explained. "We'll test it for traces of Rodenticide, as well as other substances."

"And I'll need a few samples to take to the police lab," Sergeant Weinberg added.

Dr. Feldman's brown eyes were serious as he turned to Nancy. "It's a good thing you got that candy out of circulation. We could have had a lot of very sick students in here."

"Nice work, Ms. Drew," the officer agreed.

"But this case—a sorority stalker . . ." He shook his head. "It's too dangerous. I have to call Dean Jarvis, and I'm about to recommend that he suspend all student activities on campus until we catch this psycho."

"Cancel the Sweetheart Ball?" Bess asked, as she approached the group. "That would include the valentine auction, too. People would be so disappointed."

"At least they'd be safer," he said.

"I don't think this guy is going to back off if a few events are canceled," Nancy said as she thought out the situation. "But I wish I had a better lead on who the stalker is."

"Don't we all," Sergeant Weinberg agreed.

"The tea was disastrous!" Kristin told Nancy, Ned, and Bess as they sat in the corner booth of a Mexican restaurant in Emersonville.

Ned and Kristin had joined the girls at the hospital around five o'clock. They had stopped in to see Rosie but had had to leave after just a few minutes. Visiting hours resumed at seven that night.

"We tried to get Mindy out quietly," Nancy said, dipping a tortilla chip into a bowl of salsa.

"No one noticed," Kristin said. "But somehow the talk turned to the attack on Rosie and the graffiti. Even though Fitz painted over it, some of the rushees had seen it earlier in the day. They started asking a lot of awkward questions."

"News travels fast on campus," Ned said. He stretched his long legs out in the aisle so that Nancy could see his purple and orange team sneakers. He had basketball practice later that evening.

Kristin raked her fingers through her sandy blond hair and sighed. "It didn't help that Marina Dombrowski showed up and started blabbing about how my brake lines had been cut. I can't imagine how she found out about that—but as Ned says, bad news travels fast."

"Marina Dombrowski came to the rush?" Bess said incredulously. "Does she think she'll get a bid after she threatened the sisters last year?"

Kristin frowned. "I think she just came to cause trouble. Since it was an open rush, we couldn't turn her away."

"I'll bet she put a damper on the party," Nancy said.

"That's an understatement," said Kristin. "She started joking that we were a cursed sorority. By the end of the rush, people were calling Theta Pi the house of horrors."

"What a shame," Bess said. "The rush seemed to be going so well."

"It's a good thing you snagged that candy before we served it," Kristin told Nancy. She looked puzzled. "I was sure the box was sealed when it arrived, though."

Nancy nodded. "It looked factory-sealed, but thinking back, I realized that anyone could have unwrapped one end, slipped the box in and out, then sealed it again with glue."

"Talk about premeditated," Ned said.

"Yes," Nancy agreed. "And I think the poison must have been injected into the candy," Nancy said. "The stalker must have a scientific mind. He or she can rig an electrical switch, locate a syringe and poison, cut brake lines . . ." Her voice trailed off as she thought of Max and Casey. "Ned, do you know what Casey's major is?"

He gulped, then answered hesitantly, "Chemistry. He wants to be a science teacher."

Nancy's blue eyes flashed with interest. "We'd better pay him a visit tomorrow. I'd like to check out his room in the dorm."

"Breaking and entering, Nan?" Ned asked.

"I'd rather not," she said. "Can you talk your way in?"

Ned shifted uncomfortably. "I feel like a traitor. He's my teammate. But if he's the stalker, he has to be stopped. We can go by his dorm in the morning."

"Okay," Nancy said. "And I want to check the handwriting on the secret admirer's card when we get back to the house. I need to know if that poisoned candy came from Cupid."

"I saw that card," Kristin said. "Are you talking about matching the handwriting?" When Nancy nodded, Kristin shook her head. "It won't work. The secret admirer used a typewriter. I remember it because it struck me as strange at first. Then I just figured he didn't want to give himself away by his handwriting."

"Hmm," Nancy said thoughtfully. "If the candy was from Cupid, he or she was clever enough to think ahead. We never would have touched the poisoned candy if we knew it came from him."

"Rat poison!" Bess shivered. "That's disgusting."

"Can we change the subject?" Ned asked as their waiter approached and began serving sizzling fajitas and steaming rice and beans. "I'd hate to lose my appetite."

"Good idea," Nancy said as she dug into her chicken fajita.

After they finished eating, Ned headed to Emerson for basketball practice, and the three girls walked back to the hospital.

"I wonder if Mindy's been checked into Rosie's room yet," Bess said as they stepped off the elevator on the second floor.

Glancing down the hall, Nancy noticed someone dressed in a green surgical gown and mask. "That's weird," she said aloud. What would a surgeon be doing on this floor? The operating rooms were upstairs. Perhaps the surgeon was just checking on a patient, she thought.

But when Nancy saw the man pause at the door to Rosie's room, she was even more curious. He stared at the ground, as if nervous, then pushed the door open and stepped over the threshold.

That was when Nancy noticed the purple and orange hightop sneakers under his green gown.

That was no surgeon! It was Casey Thompson —and he was sneaking into Rosie's room!

Chapter

Eleven

"Casey!" Nancy shouted after him, but he'd already ducked inside.

"Where?" Bess asked, blinking.

Nancy was already running down the corridor when she shouted, "In Rosie's room!" Her shoes squeaked against the linoleum floor as she went.

Nancy pushed open the door to the room. Bess and Kristin were right behind her. Casey was standing at Rosie's bedside. Both he and Rosie seemed shocked by the girls' intrusion.

"What are you doing here, Casey?" Nancy asked.

He pulled off the green surgical mask and shrugged. "I know this must look pretty silly, but I wanted to see Rosie, and I was afraid someone would recognize me. So I snatched this disguise from the closet down the hall."

"The police told you to stay away from Rosie," Kristin reminded him, *"completely."*

"That's true," Rosie said, wagging a finger at him. "You're breaking the law—although I'm glad you came to see me."

"I wanted to apologize," Casey said, squeezing Rosie's hand. "I was a jerk to argue with you the other night. I'm so sorry you got hurt. If only I'd been there . . ."

Nancy rolled her eyes. Romance was wonderful, but there was a stalker on the loose!

The girls hung back while Rosie and Casey talked, though Nancy picked up bits and pieces of the conversation. "I've been too possessive," Casey admitted. "Can you forgive me?"

"If you want to be my boyfriend, some things have to change," Rosie said firmly.

Casey mumbled something and then sat down on the bed beside Rosie, still holding her hand.

By the time Casey left, Nancy sensed that the couple had begun to patch up their relationship. Nancy was torn between rooting for Casey and feeling that she was right to be protecting Rosie from him.

"You know," Nancy told Rosie, "the police still think Casey might be the person who attacked you. And he might be the Theta Pi stalker." The girls told her what had been happening in and around the sorority house.

"That's horrible!" Rosie said. "But it's not

Casey. He has a bad temper, but he's not vicious."

"Please," Nancy told Rosie, "don't let down your guard until this investigation is over."

Nancy and Rosie were still talking when Mindy was wheeled into the room and helped into the bed beside Rosie's. The girls stayed until Mindy was settled in, then drove back to Emerson College.

The Theta Pi house was quiet as the three girls traipsed in. The flickering light in the den indicated that the TV was on. There they found a few of the sisters curled up on the sofa and floor, sharing a big bowl of popcorn.

Bess looked down at her red outfit, then nodded toward the stairs. "I'm going to change into my sweatsuit and hang out down here."

Nancy nodded. "Sounds like a good idea." On the way up the stairs, Nancy turned to Kristin and asked, "Can we go over the records of girls who wanted to pledge Theta Pi in the last few years? Maybe a rejected rushee has something to do with the attacks."

"Sure," Kristin agreed. "I'll ask Denise to join us, since she was rush chairperson last year. She has all the old files in her room."

Ten minutes later Nancy and Kristin were sitting in their room, going through index cards with Denise Slavin.

"The Panhellenic Council asks us to give them

a list of all the girls who attend our rushes, all the girls who receive bids—stuff like that," Denise explained.

"I'm interested in Marina Dombrowski—or any other girl who didn't get a bid," Nancy said. "It's possible that the sorority is being stalked by someone who wanted to pledge but was rejected."

"That definitely describes Marina," Kristin said. "She was a gung-ho rushee, but when it came time to extend bids, a few sisters voted against her. There was bad blood between Marina and last year's Theta Pi president, a senior named Wendy Allen."

"Why?" Nancy asked.

Kristin frowned. "Wendy didn't want to let a local girl—a 'townie'—in the sorority."

"That's cruel," Nancy said.

"I know," Kristin agreed, "but every sister has a vote, and Wendy campaigned hard against Marina."

"Hmm." Nancy understood why Marina had become so bitter. "And it's probably a sensitive point for her. She may be embarrassed about her father's job as a maintenance worker on campus." She glanced at Denise, who was flipping through the file. "How many other girls were turned away last year?"

Denise pulled out a stack of cards. "There were several dozen girls who wanted to pledge but didn't get bids from us, but most of them ended up pledging other sororities." At last Denise narrowed the stack down to three cards. "That leaves Marina Dombrowski, Jessica Watson, and Dinah Ryan. We were their first choice, and none of them ended up pledging any other sorority."

Nancy wrote their names down on a notepad. "We know about Marina. Do either of you remember the other two girls?"

The two sorority sisters shook their heads.

"Not really," Kristin said.

"I'll talk with Dean Jarvis in the morning," Nancy said. "We may find some clues in their student records."

Friday morning was clear and sunny. After breakfast, Nancy placed a call to Dean Jarvis. In her hand, she held the secret admirer's valentine card, which appeared to have been typed on an electric typewriter.

"Good morning, Nancy," Jarvis said. "Sergeant Weinberg tells me you intercepted a deadly valentine last night. And your instinct was right —the police lab confirmed that the candy was tainted with Rodenticide. It turns out that's exactly the brand of mouse and rat poison our maintenance department uses."

Nancy paused as she digested the new information.

"I have the card that came with the candy," she said, "but it's typed—unlike Cupid's notes."

"The police will need that for evidence," the

dean said, adding that he'd make sure an officer came to the Theta Pi house to pick it up.

Then Nancy gave him the names of the three girls who had not received bids from Theta Pi nor pledged any other sorority.

"Marina Dombrowski," Dean Jarvis said, the surprise evident in his voice. "No wonder Max was so hostile when I called him in yesterday. He kept insisting that he was being set up. But now that we know his daughter was rejected by the Theta Pis, Max has a reason to dislike the girls."

The clues were adding up! Nancy felt a familiar surge of adrenaline that always came when she knew a case was just about to catch fire.

"But, Nancy," the dean began, "a motive is one thing. Besides the fact that Rosie was dragged through the boiler room, we have no hard evidence pointing to Max."

Cupid sure covered his tracks, Nancy thought. "I'll have to dig deeper if we're going to prove that the Dombrowskis are playing Cupid."

"In the meantime," the dean said, "let me check out the names of the other two girls." Nancy waited while he punched the names into his computer. "Both girls withdrew from the college after last year," he said. "Dinah Ryan transferred to a college in Iowa, and Jessica Watson dropped out."

Strike that theory, Nancy thought. The next thing she had to do was follow up on Marina, Max, and Casey.

Nancy was saying goodbye to Dean Jarvis when she spotted Ned outside. He was whistling as he turned up the front walk. She hung up the phone and hurried to the front door.

"Morning, gorgeous!" he said as he stepped inside. "It's a beautiful day, and I'm free until the afternoon. What do you want to do first?"

"I thought we'd start with that visit to Casey we talked about yesterday," Nancy said. "By the way, he made a surprise appearance at the hospital last night." She told Ned about the disguise Casey had worn to sneak into Rosie's room.

"So that's why he didn't show up for basketball practice," Ned said. "He must really care about Rosie."

Bess came out of the den with a box of party decorations. "I'm going to stick around and help the Theta Pis set up for the auction this afternoon." She gave Nancy a nudge. "Time is running out. When are you going to work on *your* valentine?"

"I almost forgot!" Nancy said. "I'll pick up something later."

"Remember, it has to be personal," Bess reminded. "It has to say something about you—"

"At least make it obvious enough for me to figure out," Ned teased Nancy. "I don't want to lose out to some other guy."

As Nancy and Ned headed out, Bess, Kristin, and Denise were already at work draping red and white streamers across the living room ceiling.

"Looks like they're trying to get into the spirit of Valentine's Day, despite all the problems the sorority's been having," Ned said.

Nancy nodded as they got into Ned's car. "It has to be frightening to be the target of a stalker."

At the dormitory they signed in at the reception desk and rode the elevator up to Casey's floor. They followed the blaring rock music to room 347, where the door was open.

"Casey!" Ned banged on the door frame, then stepped inside.

Nancy followed him into the room furnished with a bed, dresser, desk, and chair. A brightly colored parachute was pinned to the ceiling, giving the room a soft, colorful look.

"You caught me on my way out," Casey said after he'd turned down the CD player. "I've got class in twenty minutes."

"We wanted to talk to you about all the attacks against the Theta Pis," Ned said. "I don't know how much you've heard, but it's getting really bad, and the police still think you might be involved." Ned explained about the poisoned chocolates that had been discovered the day before.

"Sounds like there's a maniac on the loose," Casey said. "But I'd never hurt those girls."

"We want to believe you, buddy," Ned said.

"The police are going to look only at the facts," Nancy explained. "So far your alibi for the night Rosie was attacked hasn't checked out. You were on the scene the day that light switch was rigged, and—"

"Hold it a second," Casey said. "Whose side are *you* on, Nickerson?"

"Yours," Ned insisted. "But Nancy can't prove you're innocent unless you cooperate."

While Ned tried to calm his friend down, Nancy's eyes wandered around Casey's room. His closet was open, revealing a jumble of clothes, jackets, and shoes. There was nothing unusual about the stack of books and papers on the desk.

She glanced at the dresser, where shaving cream, toothpaste, and a razor were lined up beside some plastic packets.

Nancy edged over for a closer look and gasped.

"Hey!" Casey jumped up, pulled open the top drawer, and shoved the packets inside. "That stuff is personal!"

But he wasn't quick enough. Before the drawer closed, Nancy was able to make out the long objects in the plastic packets.

They were syringes! And someone had used a syringe to inject the chocolate candies with poison!

Chapter

Twelve

WHY DO YOU HAVE syringes in your room?" Nancy demanded.

"None of your business!" Casey snapped, his face turning red with fury.

Ned stepped forward. "Easy, Casey."

"The Theta Pis received a box of candy laced with poison—poison that was *injected* into the candy," Nancy said firmly. "I'd say that makes it my business when syringes are found in one of the suspect's rooms."

"Wait a second." Casey's eyes locked on Nancy. "Do you think *I* was the one who—"

"What would *you* think?" Nancy asked him.

"I see your point." Casey frowned. "If you must know, I'm a diabetic. I need to inject insulin every day."

"Why is that such a big secret?" Ned asked.

Casey shrugged. "Coach knows about it, but I kept it hidden from the team. I didn't want any of the guys to treat me differently, like I was sick or something."

"I understand," Nancy said quietly. She felt sorry for Casey. It *was* hard to imagine that he'd attacked his girlfriend. "But it only adds to the case against you. You've got to stay away from Rosie. The police will arrest you if they find you anywhere near her."

"I know you're right," he said, frustration tightening his voice. "But it's hard. I'm really crazy about Rosie, and I know she wants to get back together. How's a guy supposed to make up with his girl when he can't write her, call her, or see her?"

"Just lay low until the stalker is found," Ned told his teammate.

"I'll try," Casey agreed. "But I sure hope you snag Cupid soon. Every day without Rosie is torture."

"What's next?" Ned asked as they left the lobby of Casey's dorm.

"Let's shoot downtown," Nancy suggested. "I want to try, one more time, to see if anyone saw Casey the night of Rosie's attack. I also want to talk with Marina Dombrowski. There's a good chance that we'll find her working at the diner."

As Ned drove down the hill, he and Nancy discussed the case.

"My heart sank when you found those syringes," Ned said. "For a second I thought that Casey was Cupid."

"But we know he's not the only person on campus with access to syringes," Nancy pointed out.

"True," Ned replied. He found a parking space near the video arcade. Nancy had told him about her talks with the guy at Video Zone.

"Just make sure you let old Tiger down easy," Ned teased as they went into the arcade and approached the guy sitting behind the counter. Judging by the white stripe that ran down the back of his jet black hair, Nancy had a feeling that this was the guy she was looking for.

"Are you Tiger?" she asked.

He nodded, eyeing her suspiciously. "Who are you?"

Nancy introduced herself and Ned. "We're trying to find out if anyone saw a friend of ours hanging around here on Tuesday night."

Tiger shrugged. "We had a decent crowd in here that night. What does this guy look like?"

"Tall, trim, long blond hair that's usually pulled back in a ponytail," Nancy said.

"And he was probably wearing an Emerson uniform," Ned added.

"Oh, *him*," Tiger said, snapping his fingers. "Sure, he was here. Had to kick the guy out when I closed at one. He was playing like a wild man."

"What time did he arrive?" Nancy asked.

"Around ten or ten-thirty," Tiger answered.

"That does it," Ned said, smiling at Nancy. "Casey was here the whole time."

"Are you sure it was Tuesday night?" Nancy grilled the arcade clerk.

"Absolutely." Tiger nodded. "You notice a guy who comes in wearing a basketball uniform in the dead of winter. He had on a jacket—but shorts?"

Nancy nodded. Ned had told her that Casey stormed out of the locker room without changing his clothes. "Looks like Casey's off the hook," she told Ned. She smiled as an expression of relief crossed his face.

They thanked Tiger, then headed down the street to the diner.

"Boy, am I glad my teammate is in the clear," Ned said.

Nancy nodded as she walked past a gift shop. "At least we know Casey didn't attack Rosie. I'll need to update Dean Jarvis and the police." She paused as something in the shop window caught her eye. It was an old-fashioned magnifying glass.

She pushed Ned away from the shop window before he could get a good look. "I've just spotted the perfect start for my valentine," she said. "Why don't you grab us a booth in the diner? This should only take a minute."

Ned tried to peer over her shoulder, then shrugged. "Okay, but you'd better tip me off during the auction," he said, flashing her a smile.

"I wouldn't want to bid on the wrong valentine and wind up taking someone else to the Sweetheart Ball."

"You'll figure it out," she promised, then ducked into the shop.

The magnifying glass was reasonably priced, and within minutes Nancy walked into the diner with her purchase wrapped in tissue and tucked into a bag. She slid into the booth across from Ned and scanned the menu.

"I haven't ordered yet," Ned said. "But they have great malts here."

When the kitchen door swung open, Nancy expected to see Marina. Instead, an older woman with white hair emerged with a tray of food. She delivered the order, then headed for Nancy and Ned's table.

"What can I get you?" the waitress asked, pulling a pad and pencil from her apron pocket.

"A cheeseburger and fries," Nancy said. "And we'd really like to talk with Marina, if she's around."

"Marina's off until Sunday," the woman said as she scribbled down Nancy's order.

Nancy was disappointed. Short of showing up at the Dombrowskis' house, she wasn't sure how to catch up with Marina now. "Taking the weekend off?" Nancy asked, making conversation.

"Fat chance," the waitress said. "She's working a second job for a caterer. They've got a big affair up at the college this weekend."

The menu slipped out of Nancy's fingers. "The Sweetheart Ball?" she asked.

"That's the one." The waitress nodded, then turned to Ned. "And what are you having?"

As Ned gave his order, Nancy took in this bit of news. Marina was going to be working behind the scenes at the ball! Was it a coincidence? Or did she need to be on hand so that Cupid could strike again?

With great restraint, Nancy kept quiet until the waitress disappeared into the kitchen. "Are you thinking what I'm thinking?" she asked Ned.

"There could be trouble at the Sweetheart Ball," he said, "by the name of Marina Dombrowski."

During the drive back to campus, Nancy was reflective. "I think Marina will talk to me," she said. "Let's go straight to the student union."

"They're not scheduled to set up until tomorrow morning," Ned said. "I know because I'm in charge of the music. I had to slate a time for the deejay to deliver his equipment. And believe me, it wasn't easy. Between the decorating committee and the caterer, that place is going to be hopping."

"On to plan B," Nancy said. "We'll drop in on Marina first thing tomorrow morning. Right now, let's see if we can find Max. We can try the gym first. He was hostile toward Dean Jarvis. Maybe if we push a little harder, he'll snap."

Ned gave Nancy a doubtful look as he turned into Greek Row. "I don't like the sound of that."

"We can't back off now," Nancy insisted. "We've got to stop Cupid."

Ned parked the car behind the Omega Chi Epsilon house. From there Nancy and Ned hurried over to the sports complex. Inside, Nancy told the guard they were looking for Max Dombrowski.

"You'll find Max over by the swimming pool," the guard said.

"I don't think he's going to be too happy to see us," Nancy said as she and Ned walked down a corridor with windows overlooking the pool.

Just then Nancy noticed that the door at the end of the hall was ajar. As she watched, it swung open.

Max stood there, broad and burly, holding a large wrench. He eyed Nancy, then shook his head.

"Ever since you arrived on campus, I've had nothing but trouble," he said.

"Hold on a second," Ned said, stepping forward. "It's not Nancy's fault that someone's stalking Theta Pi."

"Isn't it?" Max's voice echoed in the corridor. "I say the clever Cupid behind these attacks is pleased at the attention he's getting. Having a teen detective on campus is only going to egg on a character like that."

114

"That's an interesting theory," Nancy said. "But not everyone knows I'm a detective. How did you find out?" she probed.

"Dean Jarvis," Max said. "I was really grilled because of you."

"A student was attacked with one of your tools," Nancy said. "And that was just the first incident. You have access to most of this campus. And the crimes that have been committed are perfectly suited to your expertise—a rigged light switch, tampered brakes. And there's a strong suspicion that the tainted candy was poisoned with the same type of rat poison used here on campus."

"You can't convict me on the basis of that," Max snapped. "Besides, I'm not the only maintenance worker on this campus."

"But you have a motive," Nancy persisted. "Your daughter has been at odds with Theta Pi since last year."

"I wouldn't waste my time chasing those girls around," Max said. "Even if they did break my daughter's heart."

His words reminded Nancy of the note that had been pinned to Rosie's coat. A broken heart? A clever Cupid? It seemed as if Max was playing a game with her, baiting her, and it was infuriating. But she still couldn't positively link him to any of the incidents.

"If you'll excuse me, I've got a filter to fix," he

said sarcastically. "It's not all fun and games here at Emerson."

As he pushed past Nancy, she noticed a smudge on his sleeve. His coveralls were stained with dark green paint—the same color as the graffiti on the back of the Theta Pi house!

Chapter

Thirteen

"WAIT!" NANCY CALLED, pointing to Max's arm. "That green stain. Where did it come from?"

Max glanced down at his sleeve and frowned. "When you're going in and out of electrical closets and boiler rooms, you don't notice every little spot on your uniform." He stalked off.

When the door banged shut behind him, Ned turned to Nancy. "Forest green paint. You're thinking of the graffiti?"

She nodded. "We'd better watch out for Max. He's looking more and more like Cupid."

"Who would like to open the bidding on this fabulous valentine?" Kristin asked as she held up a baseball cap embroidered with hearts.

"I'll bid two dollars," someone called.

"Make that five," said a guy in the front row. Nancy guessed that the valentine had been made by Brook because she always seemed to be carrying a needlework bag around.

The living room of the Theta Pi house was crowded with Emerson students. The charity auction was open to every guy on campus, although according to Kristin, most of the guys in the room were boyfriends of the girls in the sorority.

Despite the festive atmosphere, Nancy felt an undercurrent of tension. What if one of the valentines was auctioned off to the stalker?

Brook clapped and smiled when her valentine was sold for twenty-two dollars to the guy she was dating.

Kristin moved on to the next valentine, a Walkman covered with cardboard hearts. Nancy knew it had been decorated by Denise, a music buff.

"Do I hear ten dollars? It's worth at least that much," Kristin called, then nodded to one of the bidders. "There's ten, give me fifteen . . ."

"Fifteen!" shouted a tall, buttoned-down guy. Nancy knew he was Denise's boyfriend, Larry.

"Give me twenty," Kristin challenged.

"Seventeen . . ."

"Twenty!" Larry persisted.

As the bidding continued, Nancy glanced over at the other valentines displayed on the table. Besides the magnifying glass, which she'd decorated with foil hearts, there was a hand-painted mug, a cake with pink frosting, and a few other gadgets Nancy couldn't quite identify.

After Denise's valentine was sold to Larry, Kristin picked up a white plastic bottle dotted with glitter hearts. "This valentine belongs to a friend of Theta Pi—one of the *bubbliest* girls I've ever met." She unscrewed the bottle top, pulled out a plastic stick, and started blowing bubbles.

Laughter rippled through the room. That's got to be Bess, Nancy thought, and darted a look at her best friend. Though Bess was smiling, Nancy knew she was thinking about her boyfriend, Kyle. He should have arrived by now.

Ned jumped into the bidding when he realized the bubble valentine belonged to Bess. Gradually, the bidding turned into a contest between Ned and one other guy. Bess watched the action tensely.

Suddenly Nancy noticed a familiar figure moving through the crowd. Several of the Theta Pis turned, raising their eyebrows when they saw the good-looking guy with curly blond hair and sculptured cheekbones. It was Kyle!

Nancy nudged her friend. When Bess saw him, a look of pure joy filled her face. Meanwhile, Ned had grabbed Kyle by the arm and was whispering and pointing at the auctioneer.

"Twenty dollars!" Kyle shouted out, sending a murmur of surprise through the crowd. That was double the existing bid.

"Wow!" Bess said, her eyes glistening. "He must really like me."

A moment later Kristin banged the gavel, and the girls cheered Kyle's generous bid.

"I'm going over to congratulate the winner," Bess whispered, then wove through the crowd to greet her boyfriend.

Nancy's valentine was next on the auction block. "What do I hear for this magnifying glass, sure to magnify any girl's affections?" Kristin asked as she held it up high.

Fitz opened the bidding at two dollars, and Nancy felt her stomach twist as other guys joined in, raising the bid.

"Five dollars!" said one guy.

"Six!" Ned called out.

"Seven dollars," said Fitz.

The price soared.

When Fitz bid twenty-three dollars, Nancy's heart sank. This was supposed to be fun, but she didn't want Ned to have to shell out a small fortune. Why was Fitz bidding so high for her? He knew she had a boyfriend.

"Twenty-four dollars!" Ned said, pulling out his wallet and counting the bills inside. One of the auction rules was that payment had to be made in cash on the spot, and Nancy wasn't sure how much money Ned had brought with him.

"Thirty dollars!" Fitz announced.

Across the room, Ned and Kyle were going through their pockets, pooling loose bills and coins. Ned added it up quickly, then shook his head. They didn't have enough.

Nancy was going to the Sweetheart Ball without her sweetheart!

"Going once!" Kristin shouted. "Going twice! Sold to Mike Fitzgerald for thirty dollars!"

The gavel dropped with a thud, dashing Nancy's hopes. She saw Fitz pick up the magnifying glass from the auction table and walk out of the living room. She followed him into the front vestibule, away from the noisy crowd.

"That was quite a bid," Nancy said.

"This was yours?" He seemed surprised as he took the magnifying glass and turned it over in his hands. "I thought it belonged to Kristin."

"A magnifying glass?" Nancy probed. "Why did you connect it with Kristin?"

"She's a stamp collector." Fitz pushed a lock of black hair off his forehead as he tried to hide a grin. "This is embarrassing," he said. "Since Kristin and I are both unattached at the moment, we agreed to go to the dance together. But it looks as if I've made an expensive mistake. See what happens when you play Mr. Nice Guy?"

How could she blame Fitz? His intentions had been good. "I have an idea," Nancy told him as she glanced back toward the auction table. "But I need Ned's help." She slipped through the crowd.

When Nancy reached his side, she explained the situation, then told Ned to bid on the picnic blanket covered with hearts and the Theta Pi letters. In the end, Ned bought Kristin's valentine, and the two couples made a swap.

"That worked out well," Kristin said when the auction was over and everyone had paid. People were milling around the living room, showing off the colorful valentines.

Fitz slung his arm across Kristin's shoulders and gave her a friendly hug. "You did a great job as auctioneer," he told her. "I'll bet the Theta Pi sisters raised a lot of money for charity."

"Where are my hard-earned dollars going?" Ned asked.

"To a children's hospital," Kristin said.

"That must be something close to your heart, Fitz," Nancy said, hoping to draw him out. "Dean Jarvis told me you're a pre-med major."

Fitz blinked, as if Nancy had taken him by surprise. "Well, sure," he stuttered. "I—I just didn't think Dean Jarvis even knew who I was."

"You're too modest," Kristin said, patting Fitz on the back. "He's acing biology and chemistry. Fitz is a science whiz."

And a science whiz fits Cupid's profile perfectly, Nancy thought. But why would a guy who adored Theta Pi girls stalk them? Maybe she was getting off the track. Max and Marina were still the most likely suspects. All she needed was proof.

That night the college was sponsoring a Skate Under the Stars program at the frozen lake on the edge of campus. After a quick dinner at the Theta Pi house, Nancy, Bess, and Kristin bundled up and walked over to the lake. Ned and Kyle were already on the ice, showing off jumps and turns. Not much later Fitz arrived, and the three couples competed in some of the events.

"I'm so glad you're here!" Bess said, hugging Kyle as they waited their turn for a skating relay.

Kyle grinned. "Once we finished trial prep for that big case we've been working on, the boss sent me packing."

Nancy smiled at the mention of her father. "Dad can be a taskmaster, but he has a good heart."

Love songs were playing over the sound system, and between events couples skated in pairs or drank steaming cocoa. After a few hours of fresh air and brisk exercise, the teens were ready to call it a night.

"Why don't we head back?" Ned suggested.

"Good idea," Bess said. "My hands are beginning to feel like snow cones."

Arm in arm, Nancy and Ned climbed along the wooded path that connected the lake to the campus. The other two couples were a few paces ahead. But as romantic as the setting was, Nancy couldn't help thinking about the case.

"If Max and Marina are actually working together, it will be harder to catch them," she said aloud.

"What was that?" Ned asked.

"The Dombrowskis," Nancy explained, and Ned let out a laugh. "What's so funny?" she asked.

"I'm thinking about the stars and the pretty girl at my side, and you're rehashing the case."

"I can't let it go unsolved," Nancy said, smiling up at Ned's handsome face.

"That's one of the reasons I'm so crazy about you," Ned said, dropping a kiss on her cheek.

"I'm going to be at the student union tomorrow when the catering crew arrives," Nancy said. "Want to come along?"

Ned winced. "Nine o'clock on a Saturday morning?" When Nancy gave him a firm look, he added, "I wouldn't miss it."

"Good morning," Nancy said, sitting down at the breakfast table with Kristin and Mindy.

"You're up early," Mindy said. She'd been released from the hospital the night before. Now, as Mindy ate scrambled eggs and toast, Nancy was glad to see her looking healthy again.

"Mindy and I have breakfast duty," Kristin said. "What's your excuse, Nancy?"

"I've got a nine o'clock appointment. Besides, sleep is the last thing on my mind when I'm wrapped up in a case."

"Are you closing in on Cupid?" Mindy asked.

"I sure hope so," Nancy said. As she took a bite of toast, she noticed an open book on the kitchen table, *"Hearts Aflame.* Just like the movie. Who's reading this?"

"I started it while I was in the hospital," Mindy said. "I wanted to see what I missed in the movie, so I bought a copy of the book. I was so tired on Wednesday night that I fell asleep after the first ten minutes."

"Was that you I heard snoring behind me?" Kristin teased.

"I wasn't snoring," Mindy insisted. "I'm sure Fitz would have nudged me if I was."

"You and Fitz sat together that night," Nancy said, remembering the Sweetheart Feature.

"Right," Mindy said. "We had the two seats on the aisle."

Nancy's mind raced ahead. "If you fell asleep, Fitz could have slipped out unnoticed. The rest of us were sitting in front of you."

"What are you saying, Nancy?" Kristin asked.

"He could have sneaked back here and painted the graffiti," Nancy said.

"Fitz?" Kristin shook her head. "Why would he do that?"

"You're way off base," Mindy agreed. "Fitz was the one who painted over the graffiti. He's always pitching in to help us. The guy doesn't have a bad bone in his body."

Just then there was a knock on the kitchen door, and Kristin peeked out the window. "It's Fitz," she said.

"Speak of the devil." Nancy exchanged a look with the other girls, then shrugged. Could he have heard them from outside? She didn't think so, but the guy had uncanny timing.

Kristin opened the door, and Fitz stomped in.

"I know it's early," he said with a forlorn expression. "But is there any way I can beg a meal from my favorite sorority sisters? They're serving chipped beef and eggs at the dining hall."

"Ugggh!" the girls said in unison.

"Sit down," Kristin insisted. "We've got scrambled eggs ready, and there are pecan rolls in the oven."

As she watched Fitz settle in, Nancy noticed again how comfortable and happy he seemed around the girls. Clearly, he adored them.

Nancy finished breakfast and ran upstairs to change into her jeans and sweatshirt. As she dressed, she tried to rehearse questions for Marina. In the end, though, Nancy knew she'd have to play it by ear.

Twenty minutes later Nancy and Ned were descending the ramp in the center of the student union. The sounds of brisk voices and clattering china arose from the ground floor, where the catering crew was setting up. When they reached the entryway to the ballroom, an authoritative woman looked up from her clipboard and asked, "Can I help you?"

"I'm Ned Nickerson, from Omega Chi Epsilon," Ned said, turning on the charm. "And you must be the caterer. Just checking in to see if there's anything you need."

"Cora Miles," the woman said, softening. "I'm glad you're here. We're a tad worried about the placement of this rose trellis. Let me show you."

When Ned followed the woman, Nancy stood still for a moment, trying to decide what to do. Then she noticed a guy rolling a cart of boxes through a doorway at the side of the ballroom. She followed him and found herself inside a kitchen. A handful of women were at work, unloading platters of food into the giant refrigerators.

She walked past them and turned into the cleanup area. Marina Dombrowski was there alone, transferring china from crates into the plastic racks of a dishwasher.

"Hi, Marina," Nancy said.

Marina glanced up, a startled look in her eyes. It quickly turned into a frown. "Nancy Drew—right?" She put her hands on her hips. "I wish I'd known who you were the other day when you came snooping around the diner. You're causing my father big trouble. He could lose his job because of you. Why are you out to get us?"

This isn't going to be easy, Nancy thought. "The only person I'm 'out to get' is Cupid," Nancy said firmly.

"You're imagining things." Marina scowled. "Why would my father go after a bunch of sorority girls? He's got work to do—and so do I, if you don't mind." With that, she hoisted a tray of glassware and carried it over to the dishwasher.

Nancy followed her across the kitchen. "You know," she said, "it's quite a coincidence that you're going to be working at the ball. Let's just hope Cupid doesn't strike tonight."

"I work because I need the money," Marina snapped. "My parents can't afford to pay for designer clothes and a car. I'm not as lucky as the girls of Theta Pi—I learned that much last year when they didn't give me a bid."

"I heard about how you were blackballed," Nancy said. "You were treated unfairly, but that's over. The girl who was against you graduated. And the sisters who are left don't deserve to live in fear."

"Let them quiver," Marina said, her dark eyes glittering. "They put me through agony last year. Now they know how it feels."

Chapter

Fourteen

NANCY EYED MARINA. The girl felt only bitterness toward the Theta Pi sorority. But had she acted on it?

"You know," Nancy pointed out, "lots of girls don't get bids from the sorority they choose. And you weren't the only girl Theta Pi turned down."

Marina shrugged. "Yeah, but they're not always singled out the way I was. They nixed me because I'm a townie and because my father isn't a corporate executive."

"So you went to the rush tea to stir up trouble," Nancy said.

"Exactly," Marina snapped. "And I loved watching those girls squirm when I told the other rushees about some of the horrible things that have been happening to the Theta Pis." Marina picked up another tray of glasses and sighed. "I only wish my friend Jessie had been there to enjoy it. She was rejected by Theta Pi, too."

"Jessica Watson?" Nancy asked, recalling the name of the girl who'd also wanted to pledge Theta Pi.

Marina nodded. "She and I were good friends."

"But Jessica dropped out," Nancy said.

"She never really liked college," Marina explained. "She went back home and married her high school sweetheart. We've stayed in touch. I even called her this week and told her about the Theta Pi stalker. I thought she'd get a kick out of it, but she didn't care much. Jessie never really held a grudge."

Unlike you, Nancy thought. Despite Nancy's probing, Marina wasn't about to say anything incriminating. Were she and her father planning to strike again as Cupid? Nancy couldn't read the answer on Marina's enigmatic face. She could only watch and wait.

"Any luck?" Ned asked when Nancy joined him outside the kitchen.

As they walked back to Greek Row, she told him about Marina's bitterness. "I don't blame her for being upset, but she's gone over the line. She really hates the Theta Pi sisters."

"I'll put the word out at Chi Epsilon for the guys to be on alert for problems tonight," Ned promised. "If the Dombrowskis try anything, we'll be a step ahead of them."

"I feel like Cinderella getting ready for the ball," Bess said as she stretched her hand out on the dressing table. Mindy was painting Bess's fingernails while Kristin combed Bess's hair.

"Getting ready for one of these events is half the fun," Mindy said as she dabbed the brush into the bottle of cherry red polish.

"Forty-three minutes till departure, ladies," Kristin announced. "We'd better get moving."

Saturday afternoon had been spent in frenzied preparation for the Sweetheart Ball. The girls of Theta Pi were working against a deadline of seven-thirty.

"I'm glad you're feeling up to attending," Nancy told Mindy.

"I wouldn't miss it," Mindy said, glancing over at Nancy's hair, which had been rolled on hot curlers. "Those rollers need to stay in for about ten minutes," she said.

"Got it," Nancy said, pulling her dress out of the closet. With a navy velvet bodice and a royal blue silk skirt, it complemented her blue eyes. As Kristin zipped up the back, Nancy smoothed the skirt. Her gold earrings winked back at her as she looked at herself in the mirror.

The doorbell began ringing at seven-twenty, and it never seemed to stop. Nancy, Bess, and

Kristin applied the final touches to their hair and makeup, then turned toward the bedroom door.

"Let's knock 'em dead, girls!" Kristin said as she led the way down the stairs.

Since Kyle was staying at the Omega Chi Epsilon house with Ned, the two guys arrived together.

"Happy Valentine's Day," Ned said, giving Nancy a kiss on the cheek.

Just then Fitz and Kristin emerged from the dining room, where they'd been posing for photos with other Theta Pis.

"Ready to go?" Fitz asked.

"Are you kidding?" Bess flashed a huge smile. "I've been waiting for this all week."

Ned drove the couples to the student union.

"Look!" Bess said as they walked into the ballroom. Tiny white lights had been strung across the ceiling. "They're like a million stars!"

The tables were covered with white lace cloths, and tall red candles flickered from silver holders.

"I've never seen this room looking so good," Fitz said to Ned. "Maybe your decorating committee should take a shot at the rest of the building."

"You guys did a fabulous job with the decorations," Nancy told Ned as they sat down at a table. A long-stemmed rose had been placed beside each plate. She picked hers up and smiled.

Ned squeezed her hand. "We Omegas pride

ourselves on knowing a thing or two about romance."

Although Nancy was on guard for anything that might go wrong, the evening went smoothly. A special table had been set at the head of the dance floor for the Emerson Sweetheart, and Tamara Carlson sat there with her boyfriend, Zip.

"It burns me up to think that Rosie is missing out on all this," Kristin said, looking over at the head table.

"But now it's up to Tamara to make the most of the evening," Nancy pointed out diplomatically.

Just before dinner Ned's fraternity assembled to serenade Tamara with the Emerson song. The Emerson Sweetheart gave each guy a chocolate kiss in return.

Nancy and Ned managed to get in a romantic slow dance before dinner was served. Then they took their seats for a dinner of soup, salad, lemon chicken, wild rice, and string beans with almonds.

"That was delicious," Bess said.

"And look at dessert," Kristin said as a waiter pushed a cart past their table. "Heart-shaped pastries and strawberry mousse!"

"Is there anything that *isn't* heart-shaped?" Nancy asked, nudging Ned.

"Hey, don't knock our theme," he teased.

"Which reminds me—I'd better go see how the deejay's doing. We need more love songs!" Ned disappeared into the crowd around the dance floor.

"And I'd better go check on the night manager of the union," Fitz said, standing.

Suddenly a tune with a strong, fast beat rang out from the amplifiers.

"This is a song everyone can dance to," Kristin said, jumping up. "Let's go!"

Nancy, Bess, and Kyle followed her onto the floor, where they joined a line of dancers.

Swaying and swerving around tables, Nancy laughed aloud. A couple of guys were clowning on the dance floor. She was just about to circle a table when someone tapped her on the shoulder.

"Nancy." It was Fitz. A serious expression darkened his eyes.

"What's wrong?" she asked.

"You'd better come quick," he said. "Max is Cupid! I just found proof in the boiler room."

Nancy's eyes widened. More than anything, she wanted to solve this case before anyone else got hurt. She looked around for her friends but realized they had danced off with the conga line. She would have to catch up with them later.

Quickly, Nancy followed Fitz out the door. The sounds of the crowd and the music faded behind them. "I can't believe you found evidence that the police and I missed," Nancy said, her heart racing with excitement.

"We all missed it," Fitz said as he led the way past the central ramp, then turned down the corridor. Nancy was right on his heels as he tugged open the door to the boiler room. He switched on the overhead light and held the door for Nancy.

"It's in here," Fitz said, opening the drawer of the worktable. "I wasn't sure if I should touch it. You know—tamper with the evidence?"

A gold object gleamed from inside the drawer. "You were wise not to," Nancy said. "We don't want to smudge any prints." Using the blunt end of a screwdriver, she poked at the dusty gold object. It was a chain—with a heart-shaped charm.

She turned it over with the screwdriver and read the inscription: Emerson Sweetheart, Rosie Lopez.

"The locket!" she gasped.

"I figure we all missed it when we checked the room," Fitz explained. "Or else, maybe Max held on to it for some reason. But he definitely keeps his stuff in this drawer."

"Max's alibi must have been a lie," Nancy said, staring at the locket. "He must have had one of the workers at the sports complex cover for him. And he has access to most of the buildings on campus. It must have been easy for him to stalk the Theta Pis."

She spun around and looked at Fitz. "We've

got to report this immediately. The police have to arrest Max before he strikes again."

"I'll call the cops from the office," Fitz said, rushing toward the door.

"Ask for Sergeant Weinberg!" Nancy called after him. In the meantime, she was going to comb the boiler room for any other evidence they might have missed.

With her eyes focused on the dusty floor, Nancy circled the furnace, looking for clues. The igniter kicked on while she searched, and flames roared to life in the square chamber of the burner, casting an eerie glow over the room.

Slowly, Nancy paced across the floor without discovering anything else. She went back to the workbench and stared down at the locket. What was taking Fitz so long? He should have been back by now. Leaving the locket in its place, Nancy left the boiler room.

Stepping through the wide concrete entryway, Nancy pushed open the second door and peered down the hall. The corridor outside the offices was empty, and the doors were closed. Where was Fitz? She didn't relish the idea of running into Max before the police arrived.

Expecting to find Fitz on the phone, Nancy pushed open the door to his office and looked inside, but it was dark. She snapped on the light and stepped into the tiny room crowded with a desk and half a dozen file cabinets. The desk was cluttered with papers. Fitz's black leather knapsack sat on top, like a giant paperweight. On the far corner was the phone.

Nancy was pushing the clutter aside to call the police when the name tag on Fitz's knapsack caught her eye. The printing, all in capital letters, struck her as familiar. The letters had a squared-off look that reminded her of the printing on Cupid's notes.

It can't be, Nancy thought.

She straightened, pushing a lock of hair off her cheek, then carefully opened the knapsack and looked inside. There was an Emerson yearbook, with dog-eared bookmarks in spots. Nancy pulled the yearbook out and saw that it was the last year's edition. She turned to one of the marked pages, and the book fell open to a picture of the Theta Pi sorority.

What she saw there made her heart sink. Using a red marker, Fitz had drawn a huge X over the faces of Rosie, Mindy, and Kristin—the girls who'd been struck by the stalker! Nancy drew in a ragged breath.

She'd been wrong about the Dombrowskis. Fitz was Cupid!

But why was he stalking the Theta Pis? Nancy riffled through the contents of the knapsack and found some wrinkled clippings from a Florida newspaper. One was a wedding announcement, another a story about a local picnic. In both photos, a pretty girl with straight black hair smiled at the camera.

Who was she?

Quickly, Nancy read the captions. "Picnickers enjoy lakeside fireworks on the Fourth." The photo showed Fitz arm in arm with an older girl, who bore a strong resemblance to him. "His dead sister," Nancy muttered.

The bride in the wedding photo was the same girl, but the caption identified her as Jessica Watson. He'd called his sister Jessie. . . .

Then the girl's last name hit her. Jessica Watson? She was the girl who had been rejected by Theta Pi! And Marina had spoken to Jessica Watson that week. She was still alive. But she definitely looked like Fitz's sister. If she was, that gave him a motive for stalking the girls!

Trembling, Nancy picked up the phone and punched in the number for campus security. Her mind was reeling.

Fitz had won the Theta Pis' trust, which gave him access to their home and cars. He was a science whiz, so rigging the light switch and poisoning the candy had been easy. He had offered Rosie a shoulder to cry on the night she and Casey broke up. Rosie never suspected that he would hurt her. And with keys to every room in the student union, Fitz had been able to drag Rosie out through the boiler room in an effort to pin the blame on Max Dombrowski.

Nancy gripped the phone. The first ring seemed to drag on for an eternity. The phone was ringing a second time when the office door swung open and Fitz appeared in the threshold.

"There you are," he said.

Before Nancy could react, he took in the scene with the open yearbook and news photos. In a single movement, he yanked the phone cord out of the wall and lunged at her.

"Stop it!" she cried, but Fitz had the advantage of surprise. Pain burned her scalp as he grabbed her hair and wrenched her head back.

Like a football player going for the tackle, he pinned her against the file cabinets. "You should have kept your pretty nose out of this whole thing," he muttered.

"You're not going to get away with this," Nancy said desperately. "The police know you're Cupid."

"Don't lie to me," he said, his dark eyes gleaming coldly. "You're the only one who knows." He reached into the pants pocket of his suit and pulled out a smooth black object. A flick of his thumb sent a long silver blade slicing out of it.

"That's why you have to die." Slowly, he swung the switchblade in front of her face and pressed it against her throat.

Chapter

Fifteen

Nancy was frozen in place. "The police will be here soon."

"Nice try," he said. "But I think you're bluffing. You didn't get through to them. And your friends have no idea that you left the ball. In fact, I just danced with Bess. It'll be a great alibi after you turn up dead."

Swallowing hard, Nancy felt the deadly blade pressing against her neck. Karate wasn't going to save her in such close quarters. She would have to go along with Fitz—at least for the moment.

"Now," he said, swinging around behind her and shoving her toward the door, "we're going back to the boiler room. Walk nice and slow. And don't try to scream. No one will hear you over the music—and I'll kill you in the hallway if I have to."

Nancy wanted to shriek as they moved toward the boiler room, their footsteps echoing in the empty corridor.

When they reached the boiler room, Fitz shoved her inside, shut the door behind him, and went over to the worktable. "Let's tie up your hands before you try something stupid." Holding the switchblade between his teeth, he tugged her wrists behind her and wrapped them together with electrical tape.

Meanwhile, Nancy's eyes darted around the room, searching for a means of escape. She noticed a few tools on the table and a fuse box at the same height as the table, on the wall near the door. But otherwise, the room was dominated by the huge furnace. She knew Fitz would never let her near the garden exit.

"Why are you doing this?" Nancy asked. Talking would stall him for a while.

"You saw the photos of my sister," he said roughly. "You know too much."

"Jessica Watson is your sister?" she said. "Why is her last name different from yours?"

"She's my stepsister," he snapped as he tossed the roll of tape on the worktable.

"But . . ." Nancy began slowly, trying to keep him going, "you told me that your sister was dead."

She could see his neck muscles tense. "She *is* dead, to me!"

"Why? Nancy half breathed.

Fitz slapped his hands on his thighs in exasperation. The angles of his face sharpened, and his eyes narrowed. He looked totally transformed from the lovable teddy bear he'd always seemed.

"Look, my sister and I were incredibly close. After my mom died and my dad married Jessie's mother, the two of us grew up together. We were inseparable. I even convinced her to come to Emerson," he said. His voice was laced with pain and anger.

"But then she dropped out . . ." Nancy urged him gently.

"And all because of the Theta Pis!" he burst out, slamming his fist on the worktable. The tools on it rattled. "Jessie would never have left college if they hadn't turned her down. The Theta Pis ruined her life—and mine! Now I may as well not have a sister."

"Fitz, you've got it wrong," Nancy said. "I talked to Marina Dombrowski, one of Jessie's friends. She said Jessie's happy now. Getting turned down by the sorority wasn't a big deal to her—"

"What do you know? You never even met my sister," Fitz cried, his voice rising sharply.

Nancy could see that he was losing control. He hugged himself and started rocking. If she could just keep him talking, he might crack.

Then Fitz straightened up, "And all because of the Theta Pis. I hate those girls."

There was a weird gleam in Fitz's eyes that

made Nancy's stomach twist. She could see that it was useless to try to reason with him.

Nancy tried another tack. "You planned this all along," she began.

Fitz's lips curled in an ugly smile. "Not really. When I started making friends with the Theta Pis, I knew I was going to do something to get back at them—but I didn't know what." He laughed. "And it was incredibly easy to fool them. What a bunch of gulls!"

He paused, his eyes widening with what looked to Nancy like demented glee. "But that night, when Rosie was crying about Casey, I saw my chance.

"She was still feeling sorry for herself when I told her to wait for me in the lobby. I was lucky, because there was almost no one around. Max had left his wrench in my office, and one thing led to another. I ended Rosie's whining, dragged her down the ramp and through the boiler room, then set it up so that Max would take the blame."

"But you didn't stop there," Nancy said.

"After that, it became a challenge," he said, walking over to the furnace. "Especially with you on my trail. I took a stupid chance when I rigged that light switch—but no one caught on. Then, when Mindy fell asleep at the movies, I made it a double feature. I painted the graffiti *and* cut the cables on Kristin's brakes. Since I knew all the girls were at the movies, it was easy."

143

"You even used the same color paint I saw on Max's uniform," Nancy said.

Fitz snorted. "I didn't plan that. It was just my good luck."

As he spoke, Nancy edged back toward the workbench. A few tools were strewn across the countertop, and she was determined to use one of them. Blindly, she reached behind her and her fingers closed over a heavy object—a hammer!

The furnace roared, and Fitz kicked at the metal latch to open the door. White hot flames danced wildly, setting Nancy's nerves on edge.

"You threw me off track with the poisoned candy," Nancy went on.

He sneered. "I wasn't about to sign Cupid's name to that one. Too bad you figured it out. I could have knocked off the whole sorority! In fact, I would have gotten away with everything if you weren't on the case, asking Dean Jarvis about me and telling the girls not to trust me." His eyes flared with fury. "Yeah, I heard you this morning, talking behind my back."

"I didn't say anything that wasn't true."

"Uh-huh." He gripped her upper arm and pulled her away from the workbench. "That's why you have to die. And when they find your ashes in the furnace, my old friend Max will have a lot of explaining to do."

The furnace! Nancy's stomach twisted as Fitz tugged her toward the roaring inferno. The heat of the flames filled the room as she tried to resist him. It was now or never!

Nancy wrenched herself free of Fitz's grasp. Before he could react, she took two steps back, then aimed a karate kick at his abdomen. The impact of the blow sent the switchblade flying as Fitz wheeled backward and collapsed against the door.

She scrambled toward the fuse box on the wall. It was low enough so that she could reach it by raising her hands as high as she could behind her. She banged the hammer at it, and the metal cover sprang open. She almost sobbed with relief, then stretched behind her and pulled every switch she could reach.

The room went dark. Even the monstrous furnace trembled to a halt, leaving everything silent but for the sputtering in the fire box.

"Stupid move!" Fitz shouted. "Now you'll die that much faster!"

He's coming toward me! Nancy's heart pounded at the sound of his shuffling feet.

She slipped her shoes off and tiptoed away from the fuse box. The chase was on. She was going to elude him—or die trying.

"I'm right behind you," he said coolly.

Nancy flinched. His voice was so close!

"Ready or not—here I come!" he called.

Nancy sidled against the wall. For a moment, she thought she was safe. But then fingers closed over her arm!

"Gotcha!" he said gleefully.

Nancy slammed her knee into his thigh, and Fitz stumbled backward.

Just then the door to the corridor flew open, and the beam of a flashlight bounced through the dark room. "The fuse box is in here," said a gruff voice.

"Over here!" Nancy shouted.

The commotion that followed was a blur of flashlight beams and voices. Then she heard the click of switches.

The room was bathed in bright light, making her blink. When her eyes adjusted, she saw Ned holding Fitz in a wrestling lock by the furnace. She'd never been happier to see him in her life!

Max Dombrowski was standing by the door.

"It's her fault," Fitz shouted. "She broke the fuse box. She's the vandal! She—"

"We all know who the vandal is here," Ned growled as he tightened his hold on Fitz.

"Good thing I stopped by the union when the lights went out," Max said. "I was getting pretty tired of being treated like a sicko." He grinned at Nancy.

"Would you call the police, Max?" she asked, still breathing raggedly. "But would you first cut this tape off my wrists?"

"Sure thing," the maintenance man replied. Using a large pair of scissors, he cut through the tape. Then he turned and headed down the corridor.

"You know," Ned said, "I can barely restrain myself. I'd like to punch out this guy."

By now Fitz was sagging in Ned's arms.

"No need to do that," Nancy responded, putting on her shoes. Then she came to Ned's side and touched his shoulder gently. "The law will take care of Fitz."

Minutes later the police arrived. Two officers handcuffed Fitz while she explained what had happened to Sergeant Weinberg.

"We'll charge him with assault and attempted murder," the sergeant told her. "You're okay, aren't you?" he asked Nancy.

She nodded.

"I don't know how we'd have caught this guy if it weren't for you," he said admiringly.

They were in the hall outside the boiler room when the police brought Fitz through.

He tensed when he saw Nancy. "You should have stayed out of it," he fired at her.

"Pipe down," one of the officers told Fitz as they led him away.

Sergeant Weinberg thanked Nancy again and then followed them out.

When he was gone, Ned wrapped Nancy in a warm hug. "I almost lost you this time," he whispered, holding her close. Then he stepped back and cocked his head. "And you looking so gorgeous."

Nancy laughed, but as they made their way

back to the ballroom, she grew serious again. "Fitz is one troubled guy," she said.

"I'd call it deranged," Ned replied.

"He made up that story about his sister being dead, then played out a fantasy of revenge against the Theta Pi sisters," Nancy explained.

"So his sister is alive?" Ned asked.

Nancy nodded sadly. "Apparently he felt abandoned when she dropped out of school and got married." She sighed as Ned took her hand. "I'm just glad that the Theta Pi sisters are safe."

"Cupid met his match," Ned said, dropping a tender kiss on her forehead.

"Nice bit of detective work!" Kyle patted Nancy on the back as they headed up the steps of the Theta Pi house after the ball.

"Nancy always gets her man," Bess said, then giggled. "Hey, that's a perfect slogan for Sweetheart Week."

The group laughed.

"Well, you're all invited to brunch tomorrow in Nancy's honor," Kristin said. "Rosie's coming home from the hospital then. We're really grateful for your help."

Kristin opened the front door, then let out a whoop. "Hey, look who's here!"

Rosie appeared in the doorway. Casey stood beside her, holding her arm, which was wrapped in a red sling.

"I bailed her out," Casey said, gazing down at her fondly.

A broad smile spread across Rosie's face. "I talked the doctor into giving me an early release," she said. "He wouldn't let me go to the dance, but he said it would be okay if I spent the rest of Valentine's Day with my boyfriend."

"That's great." Nancy smiled at the couple.

"It's so romantic I could cry," Bess said.

"Please don't," Kyle teased her as they stepped into the house.

The rest of the group filed inside, but Nancy and Ned lingered on the porch and stared up at the clear, starry sky. As Nancy leaned against a pillar, music filtered out from the impromptu party that had begun inside.

"I've been waiting all night for a quiet moment," Ned said, reaching into his jacket for a blue velvet box. "I wanted to give you this."

"For me?" Nancy smiled as she opened the box. Inside was a gold bracelet with a molded clasp. A closer look revealed that the clasp was a cherub with a bow and arrow. "It's a Cupid!" she laughed. "Now I'll never forget this case."

"Bring back bad memories?" Ned asked.

"Absolutely not!" Nancy insisted. "Thank you. And I'm sorry I threw Omega's Sweetheart Ball into the dark. It must have put a damper on things."

"That's okay," Ned said, taking her in his arms. "I'm just sorry we missed the last dance."

Nancy looked up at Ned as she slid her arms over his shoulders. "Sounds like we have a second chance," she said, nodding toward the music inside. "And I've saved the last dance for you."

Swaying in time to the music, they danced under the moonlight. The night air was crisp and cold, but Nancy felt warm in Ned's arms.

When the music stopped, Ned pressed his lips against her ear and whispered, "Happy Valentine's Day."

Nancy's next case:

Nancy has volunteered to work the phones for the Help Is Here teen hotline—a crisis-control center for those with troubles at home, at school, in love. But she receives one call that requires more than a sympathetic ear. An anonymous female voice directs Nancy to a deserted neighborhood, where she finds the body of Paul Remer, another volunteer at the teen center.

Nancy knows that more is at stake than solving the case. She could also save a life. For the murderer has one chance to escape detection: get to the witness before Nancy does. But to find the killer, she must first identify the caller, and time is rapidly running out—not only for Nancy, but for the girl on the other end of the line . . . in *Hotline to Danger*, Case #93 in The Nancy Drew Files™.

THE HARDY BOYS® CASE FILES